THE
LAST
DJ

THE LIFE AND TIMES OF
A 20-SOMETHING OLDIES
RADIO DISC JOCKEY

DAVID HIMMEL

LITERATE APE PRESS · CHICAGO

Copyright © 2018 by David Himmel

All rights reserved. No part of this book may be reproduced or transmitted in any form whatsoever without prior permission from the publisher except in the case of brief quotations embodied in critical articles and reviews.

This book is based on a true story. Some names and details have been changed to protect the innocent and the guilty, or made into composites in an effort to tell a sensible story. Some events have been combined for dramatic and interpretive purposes.

ISBN-10: 1986506878
ISBN-13: 978-1986506878
Library of Congress Control Number: 2018903397

To Mary McGreehin, my rock 'n' roll gramma.

And to all the DJs who came before, and those who continue fighting the good fight.
To you, the last DJs.

> "There goes the last DJ
> Who plays what he wants to play
> And says what he wants to say
>
> And there goes your freedom of choice
> There goes the last human voice
> There goes the last DJ"
>
> — Tom Petty, "The Last DJ"

THE LAST DJ

Based on a true story.

PREVIOUSLY

RECORDED

MY CAREER IN RADIO STARTED ON A FRIDAY AFTERNOON. There were disc jockeys and sales people blasting through the hallways ducking in and out of cubicles and on-air studios with bottles of Miller Lite and Budweiser in their hands. They shouted playful profanities at each other and barked back and forth about the weekend's upcoming promotions. Someone had brought in the two cases and left them in the breakroom fridge for all to enjoy. In any other professional setting, the beer would have been two dozen doughnuts. But this was radio.

I expected the place to be hushed and dank, almost delicate, the way it was at my high school station, or cramped, disorganized, and yet snooty, the way my college campus station was. This place was a wide-open, bright hive of activity. It was immediately clear to me that I was among a unique breed and that this was exactly where I was meant to be. While I found those other radio stations charming in their own way, this was the big leagues—commercial radio. This was why I had set foot in those other places to begin with. I wanted to work in *radio*.

The station was located in an old bank building smack dab in the middle of the Las Vegas Valley. If you're into obscure trivia: it was the bank used in the movie *Casino*, where Sharon Stone's character kept her jewelry. I was put into a cramped office in the back corner of the building that was shared by two veteran disc jockeys working for KOOL 93.1 FM, Las Vegas' oldies channel, one of four stations in the Clear Channel Communications Las Vegas cluster. T.J. Thompson was the afternoon drive host. T.J. was a stumpy guy with a perfectly grizzled and commanding voice and a cigar habit that would make Satan cough. Coyote Richards was the midday host who wore transition-lens glasses that were permanently stalled at dusk. He appeared to me to be operating on the autism spectrum as one of those functioning geniuses. Every conversation with him revolved around oldies music and beer. Coyote was quick to tell me about his vinyl singles collection, which consisted of hundreds of records spanning the years 1954 through 1975, starting with Elvis Presley's "That's All Right" and ending with Glen Campbell's "Rhinestone Cowboy"—the birth and death of the first generation of rock 'n' roll—and his homebrew setup. He concocted a new beer every month and named each one after an oldies artist. His latest at that time in January 2000 was called Del Shannon, who had a #1 hit for four weeks in the spring of 1961 called "Runaway." Del Shannon also happened to be the name of the street Coyote lived on—something he took great pride in. Coyote described the beer as a hoppy lager that would blow me away.

T.J. shook his head when he said this.

"No, really. It will *blow you away*," Coyote repeated with intended inflection.

"Yeah, Coyote, we get it. Man…" T.J. said, shaking his head again. He recognized that I didn't get it. "Because, kid, Del Shannon shot himself—blew himself away."

Coyote smiled proudly, and through his tinted transitions, I could see his eyes widen at me. "I'll bring some in for you. The Del Shannon will *blow you away*."

Shoved against the wall into a small corner in the back of the office, the stench of the cigars and stale beer that clogged the tiny room nearly made me nauseated. I liked these guys right away. They were radio DJs and, therefore, impenetrably cool. And if that's what cool smelled like, I'd find a way to get used to it.

A college girl friend of mine who had been working as a sales assistant for the cluster hooked me up with this internship. The job I was given that first day was researching which oldies stars were dead or alive. If they were alive, I needed to provide info on their whereabouts and their doings. If they were dead, I needed to provide proof of when and how they died and where they were buried. It was an easy task for some stars on the list like, say, Paul McCartney and Elvis Presley, but more difficult for those lesser known to me at the time like Brenda Lee and Chad Allen.

The week of investigating the dead and alive was horrifically boring. Almost as boring as cataloging underwriting rejections at the college campus station— an unpaid job I held for just under a month during my freshman year. Mundane macabre research was not why I wanted to be in this business. I wanted to be on-air; I wanted to make good radio. Grave-searching was not that. Maybe I had fooled myself. Maybe radio *was* boring, the Friday afternoon beer a distraction from a terrible life of dull workplace routine. Maybe most Fridays were actually doughnuts instead of beer. My youthful need for immediate gratification told me to walk away. I started drafting excuses to not show up: My aunt was sick in the hospital with emphysema; I was sick in the hospital with emphysema; My aunt and I had run off together to die of emphysema on a beach in Puerto Rico.

Just when I was about to bail, Hank 'Hot Rod' Hudson pulled me from the stench and boredom. Hot Rod was KOOL's program director. He had the voice of God and a physicality that was equally grand. I had always been thin, and it's an accurate description to say that his forearm was the same diameter as my thigh. Hot Rod was also the host of *Live! From Las Vegas*, which aired Monday through Saturday nights on oldies radio stations across the country broadcasting from high atop the Stratosphere Tower. Because Las Vegas was, and remains, a hub for no-longer-charting-but-still-beloved music acts, the hook of *Live! From Las Vegas*, beyond Hot Rod's brilliant jocking and heavy dosing of rock, pop, and soul hits of the '50s, '60s, and '70s, was that it featured exciting and, at times, unpredictable in-studio interviews with stars like The Righteous Brothers, Lesley Gore, The Kingsmen, Frankie Valli, Peter Noone, Chubby Checker, The Beach Boys and so on. Almost any oldies act that passed through town was invited to the studio for a chat, maybe a song or two and to witness the breathtaking panoramic views. Hot Rod and *Live! From Las Vegas* needed a board operator.

Live! was a corporate gig, separate from KOOL, though KOOL was its home station. Its studio in the Stratosphere became my new office. The Strat, as it was affectionately called by those of us who worked there, is the northern landmark opposite the Luxor Light to the south. It chest pounds over being the tallest building west of the Mississippi River, providing impeccable views of the high desert and its surrounding mountain ranges.

It was also a good place to kill yourself.

There were rumors about people jumping to their death from the outdoor observation deck, which was one level above the indoor observation deck where the studio was located. It was a thrill simply being out there, standing in the desert wind with an endless view of delicate shades of pink, blue, and brown horizon. But there were also plenty of other entertainment options done only the way Las Vegas could do. There were the big, magnified viewfinders that happily gobbled your quarters in exchange for a glimpse of the Valley and topless pool below—an overlooked design flaw I watched most users take full advantage of. Thrill rides like Insanity, which swung you out over the edge of the tower and spun you around hundreds of feet above the Strip; the XScream, a fairly standard rollercoaster car that tilted over the edge and took a nose dive to dangle you one hundred and nine stories above the ground; and the Big Shot, which blasted you one hundred sixty feet up the tower's spire before plummeting back to the launch pad while your stomach held court in your nose. Despite all the fun available to the outdoor observer, some people still chose the darker, more daring, thrill of suicide.

During all the time I'd been living in Las Vegas, I hadn't seen or heard any hard-news reports of Stratosphere suicide. That didn't mean, of course, that it didn't happen. Casinos, the cops, and the media are pretty good about keeping stuff like that under wraps. It's not good for tourism. But people talk, and it's hard to ignore a guy climbing the security fence and leaping to his willful doom eleven hundred and forty-nine feet down to become an insta-puddle in valet.

My first day up there, Hot Rod told me about the guy he saw take a leap. He didn't quite clear the slanted windows of the indoor observation deck and smacked into the one directly in front of the studio. He stayed there a moment, just long enough for the people inside to process that something terrible was about to happen, and for Hot Rod to see him manage a sad smile as he pushed himself off the window and into his intended freefall.

Hot Rod told me that about an hour before sundown, if you're looking at the window in just the right way at the just the right instant—and it only lasts an instant—you can see the smudge of the man's hand. Every time that I was up there, I pushed my vision to the brink looking for it. I never saw it. I didn't believe him, because what I did see were window washers scrubbing and squeegeeing. The ghost hand just wasn't possible. Still, I always kept an eye out for it. Just in case.

Live! was pumped through the Strat's indoor observation deck's speakers, and when Hot Rod was on-air, tourists turned their backs to the expansive desert and congregated around the thick, soundproof windows to peer into the small studio. Radio was designed to be heard, not seen. Watching a radio show unfold manipulated your perception into true reality. The sounds and the actions you heard from your car or home or cubicle were immediately wholly different; otherworldly. I had seen radio shows before. I had been on them. But seeing a real pro like Hot Rod jock a show like *Live! From Las Vegas* changed the way I listened to the radio and the way I looked at, well, everything. Because even radio could be a visual spectacle, and it never needed flashy lights or special effects. All it needed was personality. I saw my wonder in the eyes of the tourists in the Strat as they peered through the glass of our soundproof fishbowl. Watching the radio show was the most thrilling ride the Strat could offer.

That first day, I was told to meet Hot Rod at the Strat studio at four-thirty in the afternoon. I looked like a nervous fanboy standing outside of the locked studio door in my KOOL T-shirt politely tucked into my jeans. Hot Rod arrived a few minutes before five o'clock with two beers he'd grabbed from the observation deck snack stand located around the bend from the studio. He asked me to hold them while he fished through his shoulder bag for the keys. Once inside, he placed the beers on the console and organized his papers full of show content, which included the dead-or-alive work I had done that week. Once situated, he swigged back half of his beer in one guzzle. He gestured to the other cup.

"You're twenty-one, right?" he asked through a hefty belch.

"I will be in five months."

"Close enough. That's for you."

"Really?"

"Look brother, if you can't do this drunk, then you can't do this at all."

MY DESIRE TO BE A RADIO DJ began back when I landed my own show on my high school's radio station in a south suburb of Chicago in the late '90s. I was the only show host who hadn't taken any broadcasting classes. I simply auditioned and landed the part. My shift was every Thursday night from eight to nine o'clock. Because I hadn't taken any classes, I didn't understand the intricacies of the medium and knew nothing about running the board or actually producing a show, but I knew how to run my mouth. I was assigned a producer, a friend of mine who was in the broadcast program. He was as much into the no-plan–plan kind of show as I was. We made a good team. We had no problem blowing out a song or two on the playlist, which was predetermined by the station's faculty moderator, in exchange for something from our own punk rock CD collections. The one rule we did have was to replace the song "Lovefool" by The Cardigans with Tracy Chapman's "Fast Car." We did this because a) at that time, "Lovefool" was grossly overplayed and b) "Fast Car" is brilliant, folk-pop-rock perfection.

I loved being on-air. It was exciting to never have even the closest idea of what I was going to say until I started saying it. I once actually read from the Yellow Pages and improvised a mock ad for my attorney father with whom I had been having an intense adult/teenager fight for three weeks running. "Getting divorced? Call Paul J. Aaronson, Attorney at Law. He'll get you more than what you deserve because he hates his firstborn son and uses that hatred to screw over your soon-to-be-ex. Paul J. Aaronson—the Family Lawyer." I talked a lot of smack to the boyfriend of a girl I liked without ever saying his name but getting excessively specific. If he had been listening, I would have known because he would have likely beat the shit out of me in the school's parking lot. I interviewed imaginary guests conjured up by my doing dumb voices. It was 1997, and the *Star Wars* movies were being rereleased in theaters. Being a part of the zeitgeist, I regularly hosted Chewbacca in the studio. He was a temperamental guest, but I mostly blame myself for that. And not just because I was the one doing Chewbacca but because I was a terrible interviewer and antagonized him; questioning him about why he didn't have more lines in the films or why he didn't wear pants. My high school show was an exercise in absurdity and a total basking in the joy of hearing the sound of my own voice through the headphones.

When I was kicked off the air a few weeks before graduation—after an anonymous underwriter complained to the faculty moderator and student station director that my show was too inappropriate—I wanted to be a radio jock even more. This was around the time that Howard Stern's movie *Private Parts* was out, and I took the firing as a sign that I was destined for greatness just like Howard. And if sponsors were complaining about my reading of the Yellow Pages or the faux interviews I was having with a wookie then I had no choice but to become a media god.

However, I learned shortly after my firing that it hadn't really been an underwriter who had complained but a malevolent fellow DJ posing as the upset sponsor who was jealous that my show was attracting listeners and callers. By the time this was found out, I was a week away from graduation, and my high school radio career was over. The envy and malice of that other student jock only fueled my desire to be a massive success on the airwaves, and it showed me that, in a way, I had exactly what it took to succeed.

IN THE STRATOSPHERE'S STUDIO, I watched Hot Rod work, taking notes of every single move he made, everything he said, and the way he said it. He walked me through the process of show production, and I soaked it up with a level of attention and interest I'd never had about anything before. Hot Rod stood over six feet tall and had to weigh around three hundred pounds, so he demanded physical space. When you coupled his body size with the magnitude of his voice and his personality, it was a wonder that there was ever any room left in that small studio for me or the guests. His sausage-link fingers danced across the board the way Liberace's would across piano keys as they brought levels up and down and pressed buttons and computer keyboard keys that fired off the next song or a promo or a phone call. He bounced around in the chair like a wild child hopped up on Fun Dip candy and Mountain Dew. Watching him work and hearing his voice broadcast across the country, was what it must have been like for anyone who watched Michelangelo paint the Sistine Chapel. But, you know, fun.

I never went back to researching dead or alive oldies stars. Hot Rod introduced me to the audio board and the computer program that played and stored all the songs and jingles and liners and commercials. He was grooming me to be a radio producer. He taught me how to run the board, take and edit phone calls, field requests and more.

He showed me the finesse required to produce a top-rated nationally syndicated radio program. Eventually, once I was comfortable on the board and he was confident in my abilities, he relinquished control to let me produce the show while he talked. It was the exact opposite of the role I played on my high school show. Being at the controls was exhilarating. With my fingers on the buttons, I could *feel* the show as well as hear it. We were making incredible radio together, and I was having the time of my life drinking beer, joking around with Rich Little, the guys from The Tokens, and Ron Dante (the creative force behind The Archies and The Detergents) and other stars from before my time but now a significant part of my life.

Hot Rod, though happily married with five kids, would sometimes send me out to the observation decks to recruit cute tourist girls to be on-air with us. I'd approach them and say, "Hi, how'd you like to be on the radio?" They all jumped at the chance. In the studio, Hot Rod asked them where they were from, quizzed them a bit about their hometown and grilled them on what kind of trouble they were getting into in Las Vegas. Then he'd take a request from them and send them on their way. *Live!* was nothing without lively interaction with guests. If we didn't have a star in the booth, we turned yokels from Anytown, U.S.A., into the stars. And when some retired vet or aging menopausal housewife or teenage vintage-music geek heard some people from their town on the radio all the way from Las Vegas, well, they'd want to visit and then come to the Stratosphere and meet Hot Rod and hopefully get their chance to be a star on the radio, too.

Why cute girls? Because we liked cute girls. For Hot Rod, it was harmless flirting—good fun for the sake of the business. But for me, I was twenty years old and single, so every flirt was dead serious business. I never knew when I might meet the woman of my dreams, my future wife, or just a girl to make out with after the show because I was the radio guy. Often, Hot Rod would have me talk on the show, which was a fantastic rush. He referred to me as Producer Dave. And Producer Dave was cool, confident, charismatic. I never met my dream girl or my wife there, but it was fun to entertain the idea. It was showbiz, man.

Sometimes, I'd slyly record those segments on the digital editor we used to tape the phone calls just so I could listen back to hear how I sounded on the air. Was my voice good enough? Was I clever enough? Or, holy shit!—I was on the radio!

I showed up to the studio on my twenty-first birthday to a case of Miller Lite set on the host chair with a note from Hot Rod and the rest of the KOOL staff: "Happy birthday, Dave! Drink responsibly and avoid dead air!" The studio line rang. It was Hot Rod.

"Happy birthday, Doc!" he said with the same gusto he used on-air.

"Doc?"

"I've decided that that's your name now. Dr. Dave. If you're going to work in this business, you're going to need a real kickass name. Like… Dr. Dave Maxwell. That's it. That's my gift to you, your radio name. And that beer. Don't drink all of it tonight. Happy birthday, Dr. Dave Maxwell!"

Hardly anyone used their real names in radio and now I was among the ranks. I had been baptized. It was the greatest birthday present I'd ever received—acceptance into a world of excitement and boundless possibilities. I had a radio name. Something not as restrictive as Producer Dave. I was now a doctor. Of what? Of music? Of rock 'n' roll? Of podiatry? It didn't matter. Alliteration is what mattered—it sounded good. Having a radio name meant I was a *radio personality*. Dr. Dave was cooler, more confident, more charismatic than even Producer Dave. Equipped with my radio name, I could envision my future, a successful future, for the first time with absolute clarity.

Hot Rod told me he wasn't coming in for the show that night. He had prerecorded it earlier that day, and it was all loaded up into the computer system, Prophet. All I had to do was produce the show like normal, just without a live jock there. The birthday beer helped steel my nerves as I ran the show by myself for the first time. I only managed to allow seven seconds of dead air to slip through, which feels like a fucking eternity when you're trapped in a fishbowl of a radio studio more than one thousand feet above the ground with hundreds of thousands of your countrymen listening to you and unsure what to do but wait for the next song to automatically start.

Month after month, Hot Rod showed up less and less, having prerecorded most of the shows. If there was an interview, the guests would come to the studio for an hour or two, Hot Rod would jock the show live, conduct the interview, take a few requests and then head home to his wife and kids, leaving me at the digital helm. That meant that fewer and fewer guests were being booked, or their interviews were taking place much earlier in the day or days before air-time. My job was to push the buttons, take some calls to keep up appearances and explain to the caller that Hot Rod was using the bathroom or cueing up the next record or busy with any other phony reason I could think of. Two loyal listeners and regular callers made it difficult to keep up the act. Gail, from Des Moines, had the voice of a drunk and breathy Marilyn Monroe. "Hi, Dr. Dave, where's Hanky Hot Rod?" I'd give her an excuse and she'd push through her disappointment by confiding in me about her digestion troubles. "I've got what you might call... the Las Vegas trots." And there was Bill from Milwaukee. When I asked how he was doing, he'd always reply, "Well, Dave... I got into another fight with a case of Miller. Don't think I'm gonna win this one." Bill called three or four times a night. He started out funny, but each call was sadder and drunker, often involving stories about hunting with his son followed by a request for anything by Elvis. I got the feeling he and his son were estranged and that Elvis' music was the one thing they never fought about. Sometimes I was able to slip a song in there for him.

My name was Dr. Dave, but technically, I was Board Babysitter Dave.

It was called voicetracking, and it had its benefits. Jocks could prerecord a few breaks ahead of schedule and buy themselves time for a long bathroom or smoke break or to cut out early from a night shift to meet up with friends or go home to bed. Its main purpose was not for the convenience of the DJ. It was a way for radio stations to cut back jock hours and, therefore, save money. This was good news for me because as the board op, I was brought in to handle remote call-ins. This was when another DJ would be at a location, like a car dealership, and would make four, sixty-second reports from that location as part of a promotion or sales upgrade. "Come on down to Desert Volkswagen and take advantage of the incredible deals! We're also giving away tickets to see The Righteous Brothers at the Orleans!" I needed to be in the studio to turn on the remote feed and bring up the level following the voicetracked cue and then turn the feed off and manually head in to the next automated run. At ten bucks an hour, I was a much more affordable option that having the actual jock, making thirty-five grand plus benefits, being there. Voicetracking was the future of radio, and I was given the charge to manage it and help perfect it.

With all the voicetracking, I had a lot of down time alone in the studio. Listening to the oldies, I used that time to read the *Billboard Book of Top 40 Hits*. Made up of the history of music and the laws of what defined chart toppers, this book became my bible. It filled me with knowledge and opened my eyes to information and stats that would bore most people, but I couldn't get enough. I read that book cover to cover, over and over. I specialized my studies in what I knew the least about—the oldies, KOOL's format, music mostly between 1955 and 1972. Pretty soon, I had more knowledge of the format than the people who grew up listening to it. I was never that great of a student in school, but when it came to radio, I retained everything I learned and always craved more. It wasn't enough that I knew that the name Herman's Hermit came from the Bullwinkle cartoon or that "Rock the Boat" by The Hues Corporation—named after Howard Hughes—is considered the first disco song to hit #1 or that Marvin Gaye started his career as a session drummer at Motown. The details of my music knowledge drilled down to the years, months, and in some cases, weeks, that songs hit and peaked on the charts. I knew where bands were formed, what labels they were on, who produced them, when original members died—I could even tell you where they were buried—and so on and so forth. I could rattle off music trivia gleaned from that book the way your crazy evangelical grandmother rattled off scripture. I could out-trivia most people. I even managed to stump Coyote a few times. Yes, I was, in fact, a doctor of rock 'n' roll.

Even during the down times of board babysitting, I was never bored. Simply being in the studio was fascinating for me. As I fell more and more in love with the wild excitement of it all, I learned about the warts of radio; that the big companies, which owned and operated the stations, were less interested in the product and more interested in what they could squeeze out of it by giving as little back as possible. I saw it firsthand when *Live! From Las Vegas* was canceled. Too expensive, not enough affiliates, we were told. Playing a syndicated show instead of producing one was one way of saving some coin, so another company's syndicated oldies show was pumped through the airwaves on Saturday nights. It lacked the enthusiasm *Live!* had even during its most voicetracked moments, but it meant more work and money for me because Saturday nights were big with remotes and station events. The studio in the Strat was stripped down and boarded up. I moved down to the main KOOL studio in the old bank.

In a further effort to save money, Hot Rod was required to not only manage the station but host the midday shift—voicetracked, of course. Coyote was moved to the weekday evenings—another voicetracked shift. The move to voicetrack and its cost cuts forced out a half-retired radio vet named Big Daddy Monroe who had always done the overnight show live. Overnights in a sleepless town like Las Vegas were not the dustbin daypart like they were in other markets. Big Daddy had loyal listeners and took requests and played trivia games and doled out prizes just the same as T.J.'s afternoon drive show. With *Live! From Las Vegas* dead, *The Big Daddy Monroe Show*, in my young DJ's opinion, was the most exciting entertainment option in Las Vegas. Asking him to prerecord his show, stripping it of its personality, was a hit to Las Vegas nightlife and was devastating to Big Daddy. Upon the news, he said to me, "Kid, the more you love this business, the more you can be sure it'll kill you. But goddammit, it's a hell of a way to go."

Big Daddy died of a massive heart attack in his sleep a few months later. He didn't have any family, so Hot Rod was listed as his next of kin. I am not sure why he asked me to come to Big Daddy's apartment with him. Maybe because he wanted to teach me something—everything with

Hot Rod was some kind of a lesson. Maybe he just didn't want to face Big Daddy's dead body alone.

Big Daddy was a good dude. He was only sixty-four. As sad as it was seeing the lifeless body of a man who had only hours ago been bursting with personality, what made it sadder was that the digital clock radio on his nightstand was playing KOOL. According to the coroner, Big Daddy died sometime around three in the morning, which meant he died listening to himself on the radio. It was, I decided, his way of still being a part of the thing he loved most: being a radio disc jockey.

THE YOUNG DOCTOR AND THE OLDER WOMEN

I WAS ABOUT TO GRADUATE from college, and the paid internship thing wasn't going to cut it. I was in need of a full-time job. I begged Hot Rod to find something steady for me. I would have been a janitor—anything to be around radio all of the time. Coincidentally, and luckily for me, the station's marketing director was overwhelmed because she had been tasked with being the marketing director for KOOL as well as its sister station and closest direct competitor, KSNE, Sunny 106.5 FM, the adult contemporary station. I was hired on as her promotions coordinator, which basically made me her assistant. And I was fine with that. I was grateful for the regular, albeit shitty, pay, and I was learning the ropes of radio marketing. I was paying my dues. My main responsibilities were securing prizes for both stations to give away on-air and help the marketing director with planning events, organizing promotions, and, well, coordinating things.

Her name was Allison Walsh. I had known her since I started working there two years before and had had a crush on her just as long. Working with her every day was exciting, and although she was my boss and a solid decade older than me, I was determined to sleep with her. Or quickly bang her in one of the studios. Just once. My desire for her was noticeable, and I learned early on that not only did Allison know I had a crush on her, but everyone else working at the station knew, too. None of them blamed me. Allison was a blast to be with. She was funny, knew just about everything there was to know about movies—she was the Internet Movie Database before there was IMDb.com—could drink anyone under the table or go out trying. She had eyes the color of a tornado sky. They magnetized my own and pulled me in whenever we spoke. Then they would disappear behind her adorably crinkled face when she would laugh, tossing her head back to let the laughter burst out from deep inside. We did a lot of laughing. Behind getting on-air, my most committed goal was making Allison laugh. She had long, fit legs that she flaunted with tight miniskirts. Her hair was a deep, dyed auburn that lived wildly on her head. She moved through the building with authority, sometimes to her detriment. The chip on her shoulder alternated between attractive and repulsive. She had a tendency to be short-tempered with people including me. But I stood up to it, and if I could make her laugh, I could calm her down, soothe her in a way no one else in her professional or personal life had been able to. I was the Allison Whisperer.

My plan to sleep with my boss was pure lizard brain, but it worked. Within a few months, it was clear that the attraction we had for one another was far greater and deeper than simply co-workers thinking the other was cute and casually flirting in the office. What was intended to be a couple of screws in the studio turned into a three-year on-again/off-again relationship that would break my heart and cause me emotional dysmorphia, self-loathing at near catastrophic levels, a long dance with elementary alcoholism, and a late-night addiction to the video game violence of *Grand Theft Auto III*.

The honeymoon period of our relationship began its spirited nosedive at the same time management decided to (wisely) provide KOOL and Sunny with their own marketing director. They divided me and Allison so we could conquer—she got Sunny, and I was promoted to KOOL. I had no interest in being a marketing director, but I sort of knew my stuff and needed the job, and it was the best way to keep me near the studios and available to continue my efforts of becoming a DJ. Allison, I think, was at first disappointed that she got stuck with Sunny, which was a far less exciting station compared to KOOL. Its listeners were soccer moms who got wet off Michaels Bolton and Bublé. KOOL's core audience was more retired muscle car owners and former revolutionaries. I also think she was threatened by my promotion and disappointed that she no longer had professional control over me. It didn't occur to her that I couldn't have even begun to manage the role without her having taught me everything she knew about marketing a radio station. I relished it because it evened out our relationship. But because of my obvious joy, Allison came to resent me even more. And despite what your feuding parents told themselves, resentment does not make for a quality relationship.

We forced the fun and seized on the peaceful times with trips to Lake Powell and the Grand Canyon, and explored new dining and bar offerings throughout the Valley. At nearly every single turn, we'd find ourselves in some sort of fight over I don't know what. Asked by a friend what my plans were one weekend, I responded, "I don't know. Probably grab some sushi with Allison and fight." But the blame was not all Allison's. I was twenty-two years old and my own kind of lunatic. I knew early on that I should have gotten out of the relationship, but the negative energy became my dope, and I became a fiend.

But this isn't about me and Allison. This is about radio. Right?

ONE DAY, I OVERHEARD T.J. complaining to Hot Rod about having to jock the afternoons and voicetrack the weekend overnights. It was too much prep, not enough money, he didn't have the time, etc. T.J. was a great guy but had come from the days when radio was turntables and cocaine, and a jock could make a decent living working through the small markets before landing in a big one just about the time he lost his hearing and had to hang up the headphones. T.J. was a dinosaur, and the meteor was coming for him. He was worn out. I, however, was a new species, and the world was my evolutionary oyster.

T.J. walked out of Hot Rod's office grumbling an old man's grumble, and I walked in. "I couldn't help but hear. If he doesn't want to track the overnights, I'll do it."

"You know what, Doc? That's a hell of an idea," Hot Rod said. "Tell you what. Let's get you started on some test air-checks, we'll shape you up some, and when you're ready, the weekend overnights are yours."

Within a month, they were mine. Shortly thereafter, I started filling in elsewhere during the day when jocks were out sick and picked up a midday Saturday shift and was even sent out to locations for those remote call-ins that I had spent two years operating from the other side.

One of the first had me broadcasting from Leoni's Grille, a new bar that had opened up in a shopping mall on what was then the absolute edge of town. Like all sold remotes, it was two hours long with two call-ins each hour. It was during Hot Rod's midday shift. Fans had come out, thanks to the promotion we'd been giving it, as we always did with these sorts of things. The prize pigs were there, too. These were radio listeners who spent large parts of their lives driving from station remote to station remote collecting whatever swag they could get their hands on. They were regular contestants for the on-air giveaways, having somehow perfected the science of being whatever number caller they needed to be. Prize pigs had no loyalty to any one station, but we all had to feed them when they came to the radio giveaway trough because if they ever got their hands on a ratings book, their feedback could make or break a station's quarter. I was new enough on-air that people were shocked by my appearance. "*You're* Dr. Dave Maxwell!? I thought you were forty years old and fat!" (It was something I would go on to hear a lot.) They bought me drinks, and by the time I was done, I was smashed. I shouldn't have driven back to the station. And I certainly shouldn't have chanced driving the station van back to the station.

I was surprised to find Hot Rod in the studio actually on-air. Live. He had a guest with him. A stunning black woman in her late fifties. Through the studio window, she looked familiar, but I couldn't place her. When the ON AIR light went off, I poked my head in.

"Dr. Dave!" Hot Rod boomed. "Come on in, man! Meet Mary Wilson."

That was it! Mary Wilson of The Supremes. The Supremes were one of my favorite oldies acts and even, perhaps, one of my top-ten favorite musical acts of all, and of its members, Mary had my heart. Something about the way she ooo'd and ahhh'd. Something about the way she did the hand choreography. Man, I loved Mary Wilson. Diana Ross, I know, is the favorite of most people, but Diana never did it for me. She looked like her head was one verse away from falling off of her neck and rolling stage left. That, and she was well-known for being unforgivably controlling. One could also make the case that she was responsible for running Florence Ballard into an early grave—a case I had made many times. Never overtly on-air, but certainly among the jocks and beer.

I fell all over myself before falling all over Mary. It was clear that I was stinking drunk, but Mary handled me like the star she is. Hot Rod brought up three microphones on the board as the commercial break came to a close.

"KOOL, ninety-three-point-one! Hot Rod Hudson in studio with the *supreme* Mary Wilson and Dr. Dave Maxwell, who just stumbled in from Leoni's Grille. Doc, you've got a thing for Mary Wilson, don't you?"

"I've never made any secret of that, Roddy," I said, just slowly and intelligibly enough to not lose my job. And then I shifted in my chair and looked straight at Mary Wilson and said, "Mary, I mean, Ms. Wilson, I would like to take you out for dinner while you're here in town. Would you grant me the honor? I know a great taco place. Do you like tacos?"

Hot Rod cracked up. Mary smiled at me. I noticed what I thought were the studio hotlines lighting up with calls, but it could have also been my alcoholic eyesight playing tricks on me. I was losing control of my brain.

"Oh, Dave," Mary said sing-songy and charming. "You are a sweet one. And cute, too. Maybe not this time."

"Oh! The doctor swings and misses!" Hot Rod boomed.

"How about VIP tickets to my show?" Mary offered.

"Anything to be in your presence." I leaned over and hugged her. Then I felt the low, ominous feeling in the gut warning me that everything was about to go horribly wrong. I excused myself, bolted to the bathroom and puked in the urinal. I cleaned myself up, grabbed one of my Red Bulls from the staff fridge and hid away in an empty production studio to nap it off.

As far as making a living went, I wasn't making much of one—the pay was mediocre at best—but I was having the time of my life.

FLIRTING WITH LOCAL FAME

WHILE I WAS PUTTING MY COMMUNICATIONS DEGREE TO GOOD USE ON THE RADIO, my best friend and college classmate, Ben Fowler, was squeaking out a young man's living writing for one of the city's local weekly alt rags. He'd just published his first cover story entitled, "My Week as a Gay Guy." He had immersed himself as a straight man into the Las Vegas gay scene and opened it up to people whose only knowledge of the gay district in central Las Vegas was that the gays called it the Fruit Loop.

After the story came out, I joined Ben and his collection of new friends at all of these places doing all of these Las Vegas things that I'd never done or had even known existed. Because I lived in Las Vegas, I was never able to have that typical Las Vegas experience. The one where

What Happens in Vegas, Stays in Vegas. Hanging out in the gay underworld was the closest I got to it. Ben and I spent about two weeks living in the gay nightlife—tourists in a foreign land just a few minutes' drive from where we lived.

That nightlife was in stark contrast to what I was used to. It was devoid of the usual sexual and social nonsense that came from swimming in my own breeding pool. There wasn't the tough guy at the bar in the backward ballcap or the too-cool girl who loved ignoring the likes of me, preferring the clumsy affections of the tough guy in the backward ballcap. Here, it was easy and relaxed and good, old-fashioned fun. A few of the guys would flirt with me. They'd ask me to dance or buy me a drink. And sometimes I'd go dance or take that drink, but I'd tell them my orientation and they'd say, "That's okay. You're just a fun guy." I'm sure that if that had been my usual stomping ground, it wouldn't have been so great. But I was their guest with nothing to lose, and they were hospitable.

Las Vegas had an amazing drag scene. And I got to know the top performer, Shane Ennis. Shane Ennis was a Diana Ross impersonator. But he was prettier than Diana and more talented than Diana. I first saw him perform at the drag show he hosted at Hamburger Mary's. His act was vivacious, thrilling; Shane was drenched in talent. He was a celebrity, and at first, I was a little awed by his status and unsure of why he was flirting with me. I had made no secret of my love for The Supremes' music on the air, despite my disdain for Diana Ross. Shane appreciated my connection to the music and saw me as much of a celebrity as I saw him. But that was only foreplay for what quickly became a true friendship. We'd often separate from the louder part of the party to find a more appropriate place to talk and drink and share secrets and fears and stories and concerns. We laughed. A lot. And that's how it was almost every night for two weeks. He was charming and smart and funny and interesting. I liked Shane Ennis. Really, I loved the guy. He almost gave me a fondness for the real Diana.

I don't think the idea of bringing Shane Ennis into the oldies fold ever crossed either of our minds. Though, it wouldn't have been the most irreverent thing I would have brought to the station. The real Diana Ross never performed in Las Vegas while I was there. Shane Ennis was the next best thing. Having Las Vegas' own 'Diana Ross' in the studio would have made for good radio. But I was trying to keep my night life separate from my radio life, though, there really wasn't much of a difference. So perhaps I missed an opportunity to highlight a wonderful and unique part of Las Vegas. Ben had done his part. Should I have done mine? Ultimately, I decided that it was best to not bring Shane Ennis in and promote him and his brand of entertainment to the masses. If Shane

Ennis had gone too mainstream, he would have been stripped of his greatest appeal: his underground edge.

I WASN'T AWARE OF IT THEN, but I must have felt that our time together was coming to an end and that I would soon have to return to my place among the breeders. On what ended up being our last night, I was driving Shane home, considering that we might be sharing our final moments together. I had been in a car wreck the week before following a slightly drunken spat with Allison, which led to one of our many temporary breakups, so my car was in the shop, and I was driving the radio station's van until my Volkswagen Golf was repaired. There's a certain kind of street cred one gets when behind the wheel of an oldies radio station van—huge call letters and logo blanketing the vehicle—with a Diana Ross drag queen riding shotgun. As I drunkenly but carefully navigated the Las Vegas streets that night, I knew that I would miss hanging out with Shane. And then, at a stoplight a few blocks east of the Strip heading toward the highway, with a local casino's flashing video marquee splaying warm, white light into the van's cab, I realized that I didn't just love Shane, I was perhaps *in love* with Shane.

It was the perfect night for it. There was a moon out, and it was me driving the beautiful starlet home. The windows were down; the stereo was blasting my voicetracked overnight show. Shane was impressed. We were both attracted to the other's degree of fame. I started to wonder if I could close the deal with Shane—if we could be more than just friends. Was there a loophole that allowed a straight man to be in love with a drag queen? I was sure, on that highway, that I loved Shane Ennis like I'd always wanted to love a woman. I couldn't let a little penis get in the way of that.

As we pulled up to his house, I was nervous. It was like the last night with a summer fling, and this was my moment. Do I make my move and risk rejection and embarrassment, or worse, come off as creepy? Or do I do what I had done countless times with *real* girls and clam up, drive home, put on some Dashboard Confessional and cry in my bed sheets?

In his driveway, he thanked me for a fun night and the ride home. Then he kissed me on the cheek. Soft lips, gentle stubble. In that moment of pause, it became clear; I couldn't be with Shane Ennis. It wouldn't be fair to either of us. There was no real future. I was only a tourist passing through. Our separate lives couldn't be forged into one. He operated on the fringe with the wonderful and weird; I was trying desperately to fit in with the in-crowd.

And that was that. I returned to the wretched boredom of being a straight twentysomething single guy in

Las Vegas. On my ride home, I listened to myself walk up "Yes, I'm Ready" by Barbara Mason. It almost made me cry.

TWO YEARS LATER, I was drinking at the Bunkhouse, a small downtown bar, waiting for Ben to meet me. I heard a voice call out: "Hey, Dave!" I recognized it instantly. My heart began pounding—I was overcome with oxytocin and anxiety. I turned around to see my beautiful Shane Ennis, but instead there stood a short, tired-looking bald man. It was Shane all right, but out of costume. The Bunkhouse was no place for a drag queen—too dingy and mellow—so he came in plain clothes. Seeing him like that was unnerving. I had never seen even a hint of what Shane looked like when he wasn't Diana. He looked like a turtle that had been pulled from its shell and left to dry in the sun.

"How are you?" I asked as we hugged.

"Oh, I got AIDS."

"You what!?"

"AIDS. I got AIDS. But I'm good. There's medicine now. I'll be fine. You should come see me perform at Hamburger Mary's."

Ben walked in.

"Ben!" I said. "Look who I found."

"Shane Ennis!" Ben said as they hugged. "How the hell are you, man?"

"He has AIDS," I said.

"I got AIDS."

Once we moved past the shock of seeing Shane as a little bald man with AIDS, we spent the night talking and laughing like we had for those two weeks two years ago. It was good catching up with him.

"I still listen to you on the radio, Dave," Shane said. "I love hearing your voice, but it's so nice to see you."

Before he left, he kissed me on the cheek. Soft lips, gentle stubble. And for a moment, I was in love again. I watched him walk out of the bar as this little bald man I normally wouldn't have thought twice about. But I knew that inside of that little bald man was the woman I loved. Gentle stubble and all.

And goddammit, he actually did end up making me hate Diana Ross a little less.

I know he's still performing—working the small, glitzy stages, playing to locals and enthralled visitors. Every time I hear "I'm Coming Out," I am transported to that drive to Shane's house, and I wonder how things would have been different if we had done things differently. If I'd put him on air; if we'd kissed in his driveway. Thing is, I know that anything different would have made everything less than perfect.

CHUCK BERRY'S RIDER AND A THREAT FROM JERRY LEE LEWIS

WEEKENDS AT THE STATION REQUIRED A THEME. For example, during the Oscars, we'd spotlight songs featured on movie soundtracks like Lulu's "To Sir with Love" from the movie of the same name or Simon & Garfunkel's "The Sound of Silence" from *The Graduate*. Grammy weekend spotlighted Grammy-winning songs: "Up, Up and Away" by The 5th Dimension and "It's Too Late" by Carole King. Mother's Day had songs about moms or featured girl groups like The Marvelettes and The Shangri-Las. If there was no holiday or event to celebrate, we'd do twin spins—playing songs by the same artist back-to-back, or my favorite kind of treat, the same song performed by different artists, like "Walk Away Renée" by The Left Banke and then The Four Tops—or spotlight a big artist who was having a birthday. We found a way to make things relevant. The Fourth of July was always Founding Fathers of Rock 'n' Roll Weekend.

Elvis Presley. Chuck Berry. Little Richard. Jerry Lee Lewis. Those are rock's founding fathers. And since Elvis was dead, we only had to get the other three together to play the big summer concert the station was producing. "KOOL 93.1 presents a Founding Fathers of Rock 'n' Roll Concert featuring: Chuck Berry, Little Richard and Jerry Lee Lewis! Live at the Orleans Arena, Saturday, July fifth!" It was the first time in history that all three shared the bill.

My main gig at the time was being the marketing director. By now, KOOL was in the top-five–ranked stations in Las Vegas, thanks to our hard work. It was a rarity for oldies stations to crack the top ten. But like I said, we were making damn good radio. Hot Rod was a programming and marketing genius. And our ability to create events like the Founding Fathers concert was a part of what made our radio worth listening to.

My office had once been a broom closet, about five feet deep and six feet wide. It was stuffed to the ceiling with files, standard office supplies, a clunky desktop computer that hated connecting to the printer, radio station swag, an empty mini keg of Hofbräuhaus beer and photos of me with some of the celebrities I'd met and/or interviewed; Barry Williams (Greg Brady from *The Brady Bunch*), Tony Orlando, my beloved Mary Wilson, The Beach Boys, Ray Charles, a certain yet-to-be-discovered child molester known for pitching popular gut-rot sandwiches.

I should quickly tell you about my encounter with Jared Fogle. At the height of Fogle's fame, he showed up at the station one afternoon. Subway had deployed him on a media tour to promote the health benefits of a Subway diet. I met him in the lobby while he was waiting for an intern from Sunny to find him headphones. Why he needed headphones was beyond me because guests don't necessarily need headphones, but Fogle refused to step into a studio until he had a pair of headphones. I learned of this as I introduced myself and offered to lend him mine. I ran to my office and grabbed them. As he awkwardly fidgeted with them, sizing them to his head, I made small talk.

"So, Jared. You used to be a pretty big, fat guy."

"Yeah," he said.

"As you can see, I'm pretty thin."

"Yeah."

"What would you suggest I eat if I wanted to pack on a few pounds?"

"What?"

"Well, what did you eat that made you such a huge, fat guy? I want some of that." He looked at me as if I'd just called his mother a gutted cock wallet while stabbing her in the throat. Sure, it wasn't the nicest small talk I'd ever made, but I was trying to have fun with the guy. Here he was, rich and famous and making a living by talking about Subway sandwiches and how he used to be a fat ass and now, no longer was. I figured he had to have a sense of humor about it and so I thought my question was totally fair and reasonable, considering that we both had weight issues, just issues on the opposite ends of the scale. He did not have a sense of humor about it and did not think my question was fair. But Jan, our receptionist did and so did Fogle's PR girl standing next to him. I let the discomfort linger with their chuckles before walking him back to the Sunny studio for his first interview. I then ducked into the KOOL studio and suggested that T.J. ask Jared about his diet before he lost the weight. When T.J. asked, there was more awkward silence, which wasn't the way we usually treated on-air guests, but it was pretty damn funny. While I feel for his victims, I take immense pleasure knowing that Fogle is rotting in prison, hopefully gaining back all of that weight.

But as I was saying...

My cramped office was across the hall from Hot Rod's, which was far more spacious yet still stuffed with KOOL swag, swag from stations where he used to work, photos of his family, double the celebrity photos I had, a mini fridge with chilled beer, award and recognition plaques, and a stereo that constantly played KOOL 93.1 so he never missed a second of his programming.

A few weeks before the July 5 concert, Hot Rod made the short walk to my office. He would usually just holler my name, but I had my door closed because I was on the phone fighting with Allison even though she was in her office next to Hot Rod's, across from mine. Our relationship was holding steady at the point of destructive workplace behavior, like having closed-door phone fights from across the hall. Hot Rod knocked on my door.

"Yo, Doc! Open up, man."

"We'll finish this at lunch," I said to Allison before hanging up on her and opening the door.

"Why bother?" Hot Rod said. "We can all hear you. Just keep the doors open. Don't make us work so hard."

"What's up?" I asked, respectfully annoyed.

He was leaning against the door frame holding some kind of contract in his hand waving it around in a look-and-see-what-I-got kind of way. "You ever had to read through a rider?" he asked.

"No."

"Well, you're gonna need to. This is Chuck Berry's. Come on."

He handed me the rider as we took the five steps back to his office. He sat behind his desk and leaned back in his eight-hundred-dollar ergonomic chair he'd received in trade for providing testimonials in on-air ads for the company. (Payment in trade was not uncommon, and Hot Rod reveled in it. It's how he got the pool built in his backyard and hair replacement surgery. Trade, swag and prizes helped offset the crappy salaries radio paid. I landed myself a nice Weber grill, a Panasonic DVD player and a trip to Hawaii as a result.) He cranked up the stereo. It was his shift. He had voicetracked it earlier that day. I plopped down on the old couch across from his desk and began reading.

Most riders were standard. They listed the needs of the performer, like transportation and accommodations, and specifics on their backline—amps and monitors and such. Often there'd be requests for a certain kind of bottled water to be present in the green room. The more finicky performers listed green room temperature settings.

I came to the part that I knew Hot Rod had come to see me about. "Um. Is this real?"

"It most certainly is."

"Two big-breasted, blond women."

"Yep."

"Evian Water, that's no problem, but two big-breasted, blond women? How are we supposed to provide this?"

"You know any cute college girls who want to make a few bucks?"

I had graduated two years earlier and knew plenty of attractive women who fit the description. None of them would be up for whatever Chuck Berry had in mind, regardless of the pay. And I wasn't about to use my social capital asking any of them, so I said, "Probably not."

"Okay then. Here." Hot Rod pulled his wallet from one of the desk drawers and handed me the company American Express. "Go to Pahrump and buy two hookers."

"You're joking."

"Better get going. You're bound to hit traffic. And make sure they can provide their own transportation."

"It might cost extra."

"That's why I gave you the company card."

Allison's office door was still closed. I knocked.

"Come in. Oh. It's you."

"Listen, I have to cancel our lunch date."

"Figures. Why?"

"I have to go out to Pahrump this afternoon."

"Why do you have to go to Pahrump this afternoon?"

"It's the closest place where you can legally buy hookers."

"Oh! So we have one little fight this morning, and now you're going to go buy hookers?"

"They're not for me. They're for Chuck Berry."

"Right. Good one, David. Real smooth. Just get out and go. Enjoy your whores."

"I don't think they like being called that."

"Get out. And close the door when you leave."

PROSTITUTION IS ILLEGAL IN LAS VEGAS and throughout Clark County, but beyond, it's a booming, tax-generating, safe, and regulated business. Pahrump sits just over the edge of Clark in Nye County. I pulled into The Honey Ranch. The year before, Honey's had done a massive remodeling, and I orchestrated an on-air promotion with the brothel. Listeners could win memorabilia from Honey's and qualify for a chance to win an all-inclusive paid weekend experience at The New Honey Ranch. Honey's wasn't just a place for hooker banging. It was a sprawling resort. It had a bar, tennis courts, a pool and a full spa. Everyone knew what the real purpose and the bread and butter of this brothel was: Sex. The resort and spa stuff were pure marketing. And that made it easy for a family-friendly oldies radio station to promote it on-air while giving away old plastic-covered love seats that had witnessed more a la carte erotica than even the most perverted Vegas sex junkies could imagine.

If you want to witness impeccable customer relations, rent women from a Nevada brothel. Buying a sweater at Banana Republic is more complicated than leasing out two humans at Honey's. Everyone was, of course, smiling and friendly. I was made to feel like the most important person to ever walk through the doors. I told the madam who I was and what I needed.

"*You're* Dr. Dave Maxwell!? I pictured you older and fatter," Madam Maureen said.

"Yeah, I get that a lot."

"We love your station and listen to it all the time. It's probably playing in the bar right now. Come on, I'll take you there. I'll even buy you a drink."

"Thank you, Maureen, but I really can't stay. I just need to hire two of your best girls. Blond with large breasts."

"Dr. Dave… you young ones are all about getting down to business. You ought to take some time to enjoy yourself."

"Really, I have to—"

"Okay then. Let's go have a look at our girls."

Madam Maureen flipped through the schedule to find those who would be available for the concert. She summoned the girls through an intercom system in the way a McDonald's cashier calls out your order. A few moments later there were six young, lingerie-clad women standing before me. She asked the girls to walk, pivot, turn. I would have felt guilty that they were being presented like prize livestock at a 4H competition except that this was their chosen profession, and this was how they made their money, and they were earning a decent buck, too. This was the furthest thing from the grimy and violent sex trade in dark back alleys and Thailand.

"Pick your two," Madam Maureen instructed.

I made my choice, Dakota and Candace.

As Madam Maureen finalized the transaction, she asked me, "What's this for again?"

"Our Founding Fathers of Rock 'n' Roll Concert. Chuck Berry requested two big-breasted, blond women."

"Oh, that's right! I would love to go to that concert."

"You know what? I know a guy. I think I can hook you up. Will you provide their transportation there if I do?"

"Depends on how good the seats are."

I smiled at her and signed Hot Rod's name to the credit card receipt, waved farewell to Dakota and Candace and drove back to town, hoping that Chuck Berry would behave himself and that I hadn't done a terrible thing.

BY THE TIME JULY 5 ROLLED AROUND, the show had sold out. I was able to get Madam Maureen two tickets, but they were nosebleed—we

had to pay for the transportation. Loading in that day was exciting as the three legends and their entourages milled about the stage and the back hallways of the Orleans Arena. I was wearing my KOOL 93.1 staff polo with "Dr. Dave" embroidered on the right breast, so I was often stopped and asked a question or given a request by a manager or a roadie.

"You work for the radio station?" The man looked brittle, his skin blueish pale. There were two men on either side of him, each holding one of his arms to keep him steady and upright. They couldn't have been much younger than he was, though they looked it. His Southern accent was soft and reminded me of my grandfather's Memphis drawl. I was standing face-to-face with Jerry Lee Lewis.

"You work for the radio station?" he asked again.

"Yes, sir, Mr. Lewis. I'm Dr. Dave Maxwell. What can I help you with?" Little Richard walked past us, and he, too, looked frail and worn down. The Killer glared at him as he passed. The Innovator didn't seem to notice. Jerry Lee turned his gaze back at me, his eyes smaller now, his face taut with rage.

"Can you do me a favor, boy?"

"Of course."

"Don't let that niggah touch my pianah." He and his two men went on their way.

Fear replaced my awe. Trying to reconcile what Jerry Lee Lewis had just said to me, I barely heard Chuck Berry calling out my name from inside his dressing room.

"Hey! Dr. Dave!"

I doubled back and poked my head in. He was lounging on the small leather couch like a king with his spoils: Dakota on one side of him, Candace on the other. They smiled and waved at me. I smiled back. At least, I think I did. "Don't let that *niggah* touch my *pianah*" was the only thing my brain could digest at that particular moment.

"You're Dr. Dave, right?"

"Uh, yessir."

"I was told that you handpicked these two beauties out for me."

"Yessir."

"Hell of a job, young man. *Hell* of a job. See you on stage."

THEY PUT ON AN INCREDIBLE SHOW.

Both Jerry Lee Lewis and Little Richard came alive once the lights hit them—each with their own piano. It was like it was 1958 again. Jerry Lee kicked the piano stool back during "Whole Lotta Shakin' Goin' On." Little Richard was funny, sassy and hit those woos with astounding accuracy. Chuck Berry even managed a duck walk during "Maybellene." I watched from the wings with the rest of the station staff and Dakota and Candace.

"He's a really nice man," Candace said to me.

"I'm relieved to hear that," I said. "Hiring you for him felt a little awkward."

She smiled. She understood. She turned her body toward me, still smiling. I thought for a second that she wanted me to kiss her.

"We always work our hardest to make sure the customer has a nice time," Candace said. "We always give a little bit… extra."

Dakota, who had been engaged in the show, broke her focus and joined Candace in the smiley, busty standoff with me. And then I realized that they didn't want to be kissed. They wanted to be tipped.

"Oh, uh, hang on," I said as I searched my pockets. I didn't have much. Just a small stack of ten-dollar gift cards to Jersey Mike's Subs. I had lifted them from the station's prize cabinet and had been doling them out randomly to attendees throughout the show. With the grace of an arthritic magician, I divided the small stack into two and gave one to Dakota and the other to Candace. They looked at me, puzzled. I proclaimed, "The radio station—*rock 'n' roll*—thanks you for your service."

GOING STAG IN STRAWBERRY FIELDS

—

ALMOST ANYONE CAN BECOME A LEGEND WITH THE PASSING OF ENOUGH TIME. One- or two-hit wonders, flashes in the pan of rock 'n' roll who live long enough can be relevant again once the nostalgia kicks in, and legendary status can appear within reach. But the greatest thing that can happen to a rock 'n' roll star is to die "too soon," "before their time," because this ensures legendary status. It enacts immediate nostalgic relevance and provides lucrative opportunities for musicians who have the talent but lack the originality required to make their own name for themselves, as well as fanboy prospectors who can embed themselves within the legend by capitalizing on the nostalgia. Hell, this is why oldies radio exists at all. And it's precisely why there are so many Elvis and Beatles impersonators.

February 7, 2004, was the fortieth anniversary of The Beatles arriving stateside and performing on *The Ed Sullivan Show*, kicking off the first-wave British Invasion. To promote this, **KOOL** began running a contest called Beatlebucks, during which the station gave away a thousand dollars to a listener every time The Beatles played. That was the tagline: "When The Beatles play, we pay!" To develop an exciting and hard-hitting promotional device, Hot Rod hired a Beatles cover band using the name of The Fab Four to record Beatles songs with new lyrics specific to the contest that would be played on-air and on the TV commercials we bought. This was a huge contest and ideal for grabbing new listeners. We did see an uptick in listenership during the contest, and we maintained many of those listeners after it ended. This is how Hot Rod and I held on to our place in the ratings. It was a clever idea built on simplicity. Who doesn't at least *like* The Beatles enough to listen to a radio station for the chance to win a grand? We even promoted the exact hour in which the song would be played during the morning show. All anyone had to do was listen twice a day and be the ninth caller. Being that caller was the hardest thing about it. This was the prize pigs's gold rush.

The station had a different sound during the contest. See, The Beatles had forty-six Top 25 hits, and many of those songs rounded out the hourly primary playlist rotation. During the contest, we couldn't play Beatles songs outside of the designated call-in-to-win time. What I liked best about this contest was that removing The Beatles from regular rotation made room for a lot of really great songs that otherwise didn't get much play. We called these "dusty grooves." Songs like, "Brandy (You're a Fine Girl)" by Looking Glass, "Give Me Just a Little More Time" by Chairmen of the Board and even the occasional doo-wop tune like "Earth Angel" by The Penguins. This contest made Beatles songs even more special than they already were and made so many other songs special in the way they should have always been. I love The Beatles, but I'll swap "Paperback Writer" for "Brandy," well, eight days a week.

Turns out, The Fab Four was the biggest touring Beatles cover band in the world, and for good reason. When performing, they sounded and looked spot-on. The show took you through the band's years—*Please Please Me* to *Let It Be*—complete with costume and set changes. We had the guys into the studio several times throughout the promotion, and we talked to them as if they were the actual lads from Liverpool. The Fab Four was the most perfectly constructed boy band in the history of boy bands. It had to be because it wasn't just designed to put on a great show and reel in a ton of money from screaming fans; it had to do all that as the *fucking Beatles*. What's more, even without the wigs and the costumes and the accents, the four guys playing John, Paul,

George, and Ringo actually looked like their alter egos. The casting was dead-on.

Their manager/producer was a squat and squishy guy with thinning hair named Murray Shapiro—hardly a Brian Epstein look-alike. He was a friendly bulldog, protective of his boys and his product so that the radio station wouldn't abuse them, but he also made sure the station was giving them the right access and exposure. It was a fine line because The Fab Four had the rights to use The Beatles' music and likeness and all that copyright crap. I liked Murray. I liked the guys. We spent a fair amount of time together in the studio and out for drinks during the month-long promotion. It was like hanging with rock stars. I wanted to be them the same way guys my age in the 1960s wanted to be The Beatles.

Beatlebucks culminated with a Fab Four show at the Hilton on the fortieth anniversary of The Beatles' first performance on *Ed Sullivan*. I was excited to take Allison to the show. It was a big deal for the station and a big night for me, as it was the end of one of the biggest and best promotions I helped orchestrate. Murray had set it up so that Allison and I not only had third-row-center seats but also a comped meal at one of the hotel's restaurants and a room for the night. He told me it was his way of thanking me for all of my work and for my friendship to him and the guys. This was how Murray rolled. There was always flattery; there was no amount of access he couldn't get or give.

As Allison and I were getting dressed and packed at her place for our big evening, something went wrong. Something always went wrong when there was something at stake. I don't know what I said—or didn't say— but whatever it was—or wasn't—set Allison off on a terrifying binge of anger, spite, and irrationality. Most of our fights were not as much fighting over any specific thing as much as they were me trying to discover why she was so mad while offering solutions to problems unknown. They ended in a stalemate when we would either pass out drunk, start screwing, or one of us would storm out. This particular night, I was kicked out.

I was mortified. What would I tell Murray? Not going would have been an insult. I determined that I had be there. I knew it would exacerbate Allison's fury because nothing upset her more than me no longer engaging in our co-dependent romantic insanity. I called Murray from my cell phone, standing in Allison's driveway. I pulled out the familiar script for these circumstances.

"Hey, man," I said. "I really hate to do this, but Allison isn't feeling so hot tonight. She's not going to be able to make it."

"I'm sorry to hear that. Are you still coming?"

"Yeah, yeah. I'll be there. I just put her to bed, so, if it's okay with you, I'm game for the night."

"Of course! Tell her I hope she feels better, and I'll see you in the hotel lobby at six."

Murray was waiting for me with a young woman. I thought it must've been his wife. He introduced her to me, Samantha—Sam. She had dark hair to her shoulders, and I swear I could smell her shampoo, and it smelled delicious. Cucumbers and lilac, maybe. Her eyes were also dark and almond shaped. They pierced through mine. She was petite but curvy. She wore a black cocktail dress that fit her as if it were an actual body part. I shook her hand, and her skin was unearthly soft; her grip precise in a way that allowed her to pull me into her physically and emotionally.

"Sam is an old friend of the band, Dave," Murray said, relieving me that I wasn't falling in love with his wife. "I thought since Allison wasn't going to make it, you and Sam could hang out. She was stag tonight, too."

I must've said the right thing because Murray went off to tend to his manager duties and Sam smiled at me, but all I remember saying was, "Durrr, hmmmmfph. Okay."

We had martinis at a casino bar before our meal. "I only drink martinis on an occasion when I'm wearing a cocktail dress," she said. I was in need of something fast and strong in order to drink away my anger with Allison so that I could be a cheerful gentleman and attempt to enjoy the night.

Our conversation moved easily. It was standard getting-to-know-you chit-chat, but there was *actual* engagement, so we were *actually* getting to know each other. Sam had wit and a way of punctuating an intelligent statement or a joke with a well-timed wink or small shrug of her shoulder or tilt of her head or twist in her lips. We couldn't stop talking to each other. We had barely gotten through half of our entrées at dinner when I realized that the show was about to begin. As we made the mad dash across the casino to the showroom, it became clear that we should have spent less time gabbing and more time eating because the gin we continued to guzzle was preparing a full-body occupation.

Several times during the show, Sam would look to me and pass me a knowing smile. I don't know what she knew, but that's what the smile looked like—like she knew something. And I would smile back, trying to make mine just as knowing in an effort to keep up. When the band played "Strawberry Fields Forever," she leaned over and breathed in my ear, "I love this song." I put my mouth to her ear and replied, "Me, too. It's my favorite Beatles song." She took my hand and gave it a slow squeeze.

At the height of the psychedelic pull of the show and the flirtatious pull of Samantha, I had a sober moment of clarity. Allison. I slyly checked my phone. She hadn't called. Good, I thought. But also, bad. Were we breaking up? Was that the fight that finally did us in? Was Sam my future? Was my behavior with Sam inappropriate for a guy in a relationship with someone else? Thing was, Sam and I were on a date. A date that was meant for me and my girlfriend. I began to think that I was being a total asshole.

Sam and I popped backstage after the show. The scene was Beatlemania of Bizzaro World proportions: Middle-aged women throwing themselves at the guys while their husbands looked on with mile-wide grins.

"How'd you like the show?" Murray asked as he emerged from the fandom, sweat seeping from his naked scalp.

"Incredible," I mostly slurred.

"Glad you're having fun. Enjoy the rest of your night. I have to keep the guys in line."

"Looks like you need to keep those women in line," Sam said. She and Murray cheek kissed.

"Always great to see you, doll. Take of care of my man, Dr. Dave!"

"I will!"

We returned to the bar where our night had started. More martinis. At this point, my blood was mostly gin, my brain vermouth, and my liver olives. I honestly cannot begin to explain to you how Sam and I were not only standing but still able to communicate. I also cannot tell you exactly what we talked about other than to say it was flirty. There was more touching, closer talking. And then it hit me. It all made sense. It might have been rude to ask but I had to.

"Are you a prostitute?"

"No." She laughed.

"Is that the truth? Murray didn't hire you?"

"Dave, I am not a hooker. Honest. Why?"

"It's just that I was supposed to be here with my girlfriend and she bailed and I show up and Murray introduces you to me. And you're perfect in every way and—"

"Dave, I'm friends with the band. And Murray thought you'd like me."

"That's what a hooker would say."

She laughed again. Thankfully. "You're probably right. Look, I was college roommates with Murray's daughter. We're still friends. He's like my dad. Okay? I always see the shows when they're in town. Besides, I told you, I'm a club promoter." I started to say it… "Which is what a hooker would say, I know."

There was some relief that I wasn't being charmed by a professional and that maybe she actually did like me. But then I realized that this scenario was almost worse. I needed to get to the bottom of it.

"Do you like me?"

She smiled that knowing smile she'd been promoting all night. "I do."

"I have a girlfriend."

"I know."

"Doesn't that pose a problem?"

"Do you like me?"

"I do."

"Then yes, it poses a problem. But one that's easy to fix."

"How?"

"You haven't talked about her much at all tonight, but when you have, you don't seem happy about it. You seem angry with her."

"I am angry with her."

"I know you're angry with her about tonight, but I'm talking about a chronic anger."

I considered this for a moment and then said, "I do like you." She smiled, took my hand and gave it a slow squeeze that lasted for what felt like hours. We locked eyes. "I have a room here tonight."

"I know." She slowly squeezed my hand again.

This was my moment. It was my uncomplicated way out of Situation Allison. I could take Sam upstairs, we'd do whatever we would do, then I'd take her for breakfast, and we'd make plans to meet again. I'd drive back to Allison's and pack up my stuff while telling her it was over. I wouldn't mention Sam because that would only hurt her, and there was no reason to do that. The fight was enough. But sleeping with Sam in that comped Hilton suite would have given me the confidence that a future with better women existed—something that I needed so that I could make the decision to leave. Isn't that why most of us stay in bad relationships? We are afraid we'll be alone and are convinced we're horrible people? My night with Sam proved otherwise to me. Yeah, this was my moment.

"Should we go to that room?" she asked, still squeezing my hand, smiling that knowing smile.

I had never been unfaithful to any girlfriend, but for the first time, I understood the attraction to stepping out while in a bad relationship, and in that moment, I had never wanted to do anything more.

It wouldn't have been right. It wouldn't have been fair. And I wanted to keep that faithful streak going. But I couldn't.

The elevator doors had barely closed before my hand was up her skirt and she had breached the zipper of my pants. We tore the hotel suite apart in savage passion. Maybe a little hate fucking on my end as angry and exhausting thoughts of Allison popped into my head. Sam and I collapsed in each other's arms sweaty and spent.

The guilt woke me. Still drunk, I pulled my shit together and wrote Sam a note:

```
Meeting you was a magnificent
experience.
```

```
    I wish it could be like this always.
    - Dave
```

Then I carefully drove to the radio station.

No one else was in the building. It was nearly three a.m., and as I lay down on the studio floor using my suit coat as a pillow and passed out, I could hear my prerecorded voice on the air talking about the great time Allison and I had at The Fab Four show on the backend of one of those dusty grooves, Connie Frances' 1959 hit, "Lipstick on Your Collar."

THE LARGEST RADIO PROMOTION IN LAS VEGAS HISTORY

—

HERE'S HOW THE KOOL SUMMER OF FUN WORKED: You could pick up KOOL 93.1 bumper stickers at the Miller Lite endcap display at any 7-Eleven in the Valley or grab them at any station appearances or events, or at the station itself. The sticker back was a registration form; fill it out, get it to the station through the mail or in-person at those aforementioned appearances, or events and you'd be registered to win a weekly prize—small stuff like concert tickets, cash, movie passes, restaurant certificates, etc.—or the monthly prize—a

PT Cruiser, Malibu ski boat, or an in-ground pool with a waterfall feature. By registering at all, everyone was eligible to win a house at the end of the promotion. There was no limit to how many times you could register. As a bonus, if anyone from the KOOL staff saw a bumper sticker on your vehicle, we'd announce your license plate on-air, and if you called back within nine minutes, we'd register you for that month's prize. Weekly winners were not eligible for monthly prizes, so there was a huge benefit to actually putting the sticker on your car because it automatically qualified you for the two biggest gets. The promotion kicked off with a concert on the Saturday of Memorial Day weekend at the Cannery Casino Hotel in North Las Vegas, featuring Brian Hyland, The Dave Clark Five, and The Buckinghams and culminated with the house drawing on the Saturday of Labor Day weekend among the model homes at the regional office of Masterson Homes, the luxury home builder we partnered with.

We asked a great deal from our promotion partners. They needed to provide the space, the willingness to share any priority signage, the vehicles, the parts and labor for the pool, and the whole goddamn house. We even got The Cannery to pay for the bands. In exchange, depending on their level of giving, sacrifice, or involvement, the partners received produced commercials, live on-air mentions and produced promos, a presence on our website, signage where available and necessary, and inclusion in our television spots. That was the one thing I had a budget for, TV commercials.

The thing that mattered most in radio was television. As the marketing director, I was sending press releases to the TV stations at least once a week, promoting some KOOL appearance or event. If people were watching TV, they weren't listening to the radio. To win in the ratings, we needed to constantly be at the top of mind. They couldn't watch TV when they were driving or when they were at work, mostly. We needed to let people know how great we were at every opportunity. The Buggles had it wrong. Video didn't kill the radio star; it helped the star collect ratings and advertising dollars.

In 2002, when Congress approved funding for using Yucca Mountain, located just eighty miles northwest of Las Vegas, as a nuclear waste depository, we orchestrated a protest against it, complete with a "Hell No! We Won't Glow" billboard. We had listeners come out to the Nissan car dealership on the east side of town over which the billboard towered to sign a duplicate billboard that we then had placed two blocks from the Capitol Building in D.C. Local and national TV crews were there to capture it. It made sense. We were an oldies station. Our playlist consisted of the protest and counterculture songs of the 1960s. A move like this was right up our alley.

Another trap set for TV coverage followed the murder of a Las Vegas Metro police officer as he responded to a domestic violence call at a northwest Las Vegas home. The man inside had a gun, and a short firefight commenced, leaving the cop dead on the doorstep. The officer had a wife and two young children. We took our mobile station, which resembled a large boom box wrapped in the station logo, to a Chrysler Jeep dealer, and held a fundraiser for the slain cop's family. In one afternoon, we raised over one hundred thousand dollars. The police were out there. The family was out there. The Chrysler Jeep dealer sold a few cars, and the TV news crews were there to capture it all. We were a family-friendly station. A move like this was another one right up our alley.

Not all TV coverage we got was on such massive political and emotional scales. Most of it was a few minutes on the morning news programs about, say, the peanut-butter-and-banana-sandwich grilling party we had at the Elvis Museum on the King's birthday, and things of that sort. But all of that was marketing and PR. The TV spots we bought for the KOOL Summer of Fun were serious business. Between the ads running seven days a week at least once in every daypart, and the on-air mentions and on-site exposure, the KOOL Summer of Fun dominated the Las Vegas Valley for three months straight. And everyone was happy; the sponsors, the listeners, and our ratings numbers. Everyone, that is, but the Masterson Homes peon I had to deal with directly.

Missy Lingner was a wound-up nugget of stress, mistrust, and anxiety. Disheveled from her unwashed long, crimped, sandy hair to her worn-down, scuffed-up pumps with an everyday off-the-rack skirt suit, she sounded like she was on the verge of tears every time she spoke. At first, it was hard not to pity her. I had no idea what her personal life was like, but I assumed she had none because she lived and breathed housing developments. It was clear, however, that the life she did have, her work life, was rapidly making her insane.

She complained constantly. The live promos weren't read *exactly* at the :20, :35, and :50 breaks each hour. But the jock would always read them at the top of the break, which was either a minute or two after the hard number listed in the agreement. And that's because not every hour in radio runs at a precise time. Songs have different lengths. Some spot blocks have more commercials than others. Sometimes jocks spend a little more time talking in and out of breaks. No one in the history of radio would have complained about that except Missy Lingner. And she would complain to me that the 7-Eleven displays were low on bumper stickers. Thanks for letting me know, I'd say. It's a good problem to have, I'd say. It means people are registering—they want your house, I'd say. We'll get out there today and restock them as part of routine promotion maintenance, I'd say. She would complain whenever she heard another homebuilder's ad run on our station and even on any of the other three stations in the Clear Channel cluster. But I promised her and even printed out reports proving that any direct competitor ads did not run in the same block as hers. There was simply no pleasing her.

She would have gladly gone to Hot Rod or to the station's sales manager, Bill Hastings, but she did not have the clout or the backbone to go past me. As the marketing director, I was the gatekeeper. Plus, Hot Rod and Bill both knew what a pill she was, and they took a hefty amount of joy watching me suffer as I managed her. "It'll put hair on your chest, kid," Bill told me.

In August, with a little less than a month to go in the promotion, Missy phoned me at my office in the late afternoon.

"I've been listening to KOOL since six this morning," she whined.

"Hello, Missy. How are you?"

"I'm unhappy, *Dave*." She always added an emphasis to my name as if she doubted it were even a name at all.

"I'm sorry to hear that. What's the problem now?"

"Now? *Now*? It's always a problem, *Dave*. I'm not hearing any mentions of our homes. I am supposed to hear the on-air talent talk about the house giveaway before every commercial break. And I should be getting one sixty-second spot every other commercial break. I'm not hearing anything. *Dave.*"

"That's not true, Missy. I've been listening all day. Everything has run as it is scheduled to and as it has been for months now."

"Not on *my* radio."

I jumped into the Prophet system from my desktop and reviewed the log, which would confirm or debunk her accusation. "Missy, I'm looking at the log right now, and those spots ran. Are you sure you were listening to the right station?"

"Of course I was."

"Sounds like you're in your car now. What channel is your radio on?"

"Ninety-six-point-three."

"Well, there's your problem, Missy. We are at *ninety-three-point-one*. You've been listening to the wrong station."

"Fine! But I always listened every other time! Maybe I bumped the dial or something! I always listen, and I never hear those spots! I was promised a certain amount of on-air promotion, and I'm not getting it!"

"I assure you, you are."

"Don't interrupt me! I am not getting what I was promised! I'll pull this house away! You think I can't? You think I won't? Because I can, and I will! Now you listen to me, *Dave*! You're going to run two of our spots in every commercial break from now until we give the house away or else!"

If I had to, I'd have bet that those near-tears had finally burst through. But it didn't matter whether she was crying or not. She was screaming at me, falsely accusing me and my station and threatening me. Missy was a client. She was my elder. She was a woman. There were a lot of professional and social niceties I had had to stick to, but there was a line, and Missy had crossed it. I wanted to reach through the phone, punch her in the ear, grab her steering wheel and jerk the car into oncoming traffic. Since that was physically impossible, and I didn't want to risk hurting any innocent drivers, I considered asking her to come to the station so we could talk, and I'd kill her there. But that wasn't a sound option either. Instead, I took a deep breath and sat quietly to make sure she was done throwing her fit. The second sniffle made it clear to me that she was, so in a calm but firm manner—the way an adult would respond to a crabby, neurotic kindergartner—I asked her, "Missy. Are you done?"

"Yes."

"I need you to take a deep breath and think about what you are doing. You're risking losing millions of dollars of investment from several large companies—companies much larger than yours—in exchange for some really bad

PR for those companies. And you'll lose money, too, as well as receive most of that bad PR. Your accusations are uninformed and unnecessarily nasty. I am certain that the only person who would catch hell if you yanked the house is you. You have no reason or right to speak to me like that, and you have no basis for any of your complaints. Everyone at this station is tired of hearing you complain. They're tired of hearing you bad-mouth our hard work and us personally. It is unprofessional and just plain rude. If you even *think* of speaking to me, or anyone else at KOOL, in the manner you just did, I'll personally see to it that you're removed from this account and maybe even fired. And you know what, Missy? I *can* do that. Because you are not respected here. You're not even respected at your own company. I know that's why you're so wound up. You're in a constant struggle to prove and reprove yourself to your boss. But he doesn't care. He just wants you to handle the menial tasks: listen to the radio, make sure everything's fine—which it is—and make sure there's a big red bow on the house and refreshments under shade when we do the drawing. That's it. You are creating problems to solve, but you'll never solve them because the problems do not exist. You know I'm right. So, apologize to me, then hang up your phone, put your radio back on the right station and finish driving to wherever you were going—as long as it's not here."

Silence. Another sniffle. And then, "I'm sorry."

"Thank you," I said, but she had already hung up.

I didn't like the woman one bit, but I did understand why she was such an asshole. Her job sucked. Her boss, the regional director, was a real patriarchal prick. I saw the way he treated her, and I think he kept her employed just to do his grunt work and push her around. I might have felt sorry for her despite her insanity and insults had she had even an ounce of self-respect.

THE KICKOFF CONCERT at The Cannery was a small carnival. Inside the walls of the casino's outdoor pavilion, we had the Malibu boat and the PT Cruiser on display along with the three large pool models representing the choices of shape the pool winner would have. Missy set up a small display of their luxury home offerings and manned the table all day without talking to anyone from the station and hardly engaging listeners interested in learning more about the homes. She stood there at a kind of slacked attention sweating through her dark skirt suit, probably suffering mild heat stroke in the ninety-degree desert heat. We had a dunk tank with the jocks taking turns on the seat. There were cotton candy and snow cone machines; a popcorn machine; booths trading street food for purchased tickets; Miller Lite booths pouring ice-cold pilsner for more tickets; other booths that had paid to be there in order to promote and sell their ergonomic office chairs, handmade jewelry, custom T-shirts and more.

The Buckinghams were one of my favorite oldies bands, and they were the first concert I remember seeing when my parents took me to some summer festival in Chicago where the group had played when I was about six years old. The Buckinghams were originally Chicago guys like me, so I had an affinity for them. I introduced myself to them backstage. We swapped stories of Chicago and debated which baseball team was the better. They were all fun, humorous, genuinely nice guys. They shared with me exciting stories of rock 'n' roll-inspired debauchery including one greatly disturbing story involving Tom Jones stripping himself naked in their hotel room hoping to impress a beautiful female fan. All of us being unsettled by the story—me hearing it and The Buckinghams reliving it—we simultaneously agreed it was best to get ready for the show.

Brian Hyland was opening, then The Buckinghams, and then The Dave Clark Five, featuring original lead singer Mike Smith. I watched the whole show from the wings. Like every oldies act I saw while working for KOOL, I was blown away by not only the performances and the ability for the bands to still sound young and be excited to play but also at how the audience consumed such pleasure from seeing the bands of their youth play the songs from the soundtracks of their lives.

That show would be Mike Smith's last performance ever. Early that autumn, while climbing a seven-foot gate after he locked himself out of his house in Spain, Mike fell, landed on his head and broke his spine in three places. This left him paralyzed from the waist down as well as in his right arm, with extremely limited movement in his left. He died a few years later from complications from that accident.

THE KOOL SUMMER OF FUN was a model for successful radio. It engaged every aspect of listenership, media, and sponsorship. It cemented the notion, certainly for me at the time, that radio was a lifestyle. People wanted to do more than just listen to it. They wanted to see it, touch it, compete for it, be a part of it and make it theirs. We continued that success over the next three summers. But that last year we didn't have a house to give away. Missy's precious company couldn't afford it. Neither could any other homebuilders. The bursting of the Housing Bubble was on the horizon. That wasn't the only reason the last year was smaller than before and, well, the last. By then, Hot Rod was gone, and I had moved out of marketing to be on-air full time. The new program director and marketing director weren't able to sort out all of the details. The station's ratings had dropped, and sponsors had lost faith that their investment would be worth it. The big prizes that final year were a trailer camper, which was given away in the middle of July, and a Toyota RAV4 given away in August at the end of the promotion.

As an on-air personality, it was difficult to get excited about the KOOL Summer of Fun when there just wasn't all that much fun about it. And it was painful to see our replacements let slip away all the momentum Hot Rod and I had built. It was looking like KOOL 93.1 was heading for a similar fate.

During that last KOOL Summer of Fun, I was doing a remote broadcast from the Toyota dealership. Miller Lite was still a sponsor and had coordinated giving away beer swag at the remote. We had Miller Lite T-shirts, hats, coolers, and inflatable chairs and couches. I had just finished the first break of four when I heard a familiar whine.

"*Dave…*"

I turned around to see Missy Lingner marching toward me. She was wearing her uniformed dark skirt suit and scuffed-up pumps. Her hair looked rattier than I remembered it, and even from ten yards away, I could make out the distinct pit stains on her suit coat.

"*Dave*," she said again.

"Missy. Surprised to see you here."

"I was just listening to the radio, and I heard you talking."

"Yeah, well, that's pretty much how radio works."

"You didn't mention the Miller Lite promotional material we're giving away."

"What's this '*we're*?'"

"I'm with Miller Lite now."

"What, the homebuilding business dry up?"

"I was fired, if you must know."

"Really? Any particular reason?"

"If you must know—"

"Oh, I must."

"I threw up in an office plant."

"Wow."

"I had a breakdown in the office."

"Apparently."

"My psychologist says I need to be more honest with myself and others so that I don't build up tension and create panic in my mind."

"That's sound advice. So, what can I help you with?"

"I just told you! I didn't hear you mention the promotional materials!"

"Missy, it's the first break of four. Look. Here's my script. I'm going to mention them. I only have one minute each break to promote all I have to promote. You'll get your fair mentions. And remember, we've been promoting this all week."

"I need you to go on-air right now and talk about the inflatable chair."

"I'm not doing that. That's not how this works."

"I'm warning you, *Dave*."

I walked around the table under the station-branded tent where I was standing and gently took Missy by the arm and coolly escorted her away from the listeners.

"Missy, I don't like you. But I'm telling you this in an effort to save you some serious embarrassment. I don't know why in God's name Miller Lite would have hired you. Maybe they didn't work as closely with you as the rest of us did, but if you want to keep them from finding out what a raging lunatic you are, I strongly suggest you get back in your car and drive away. Go somewhere, anywhere else. Maybe to your psychologist's office. But do yourself a favor and stay away from KOOL events. It's better for business. It's better for your mental health."

I turned and walked back toward the tent.

"*Dave*! You won't do this to me again!"

I turned back to her. "Missy, you've done all this to yourself. Go on. Get out of here. Please."

She got back in her car and peeled out of the parking spot, sending up smoke and the stench of burned rubber as she fishtailed away. She didn't make it far. She lost control and smashed her Daewoo into the steel stand that was regally holding a silver Toyota 4Runner. Her car's front end folded around the stand, which buckled enough to bring the 4Runner sliding down on the hood of the Daewoo and through the windshield.

Everyone ran over to the wreck. Missy crawled out unharmed, somehow looking more put together and calm than I'd ever seen her. As the fire department and police assessed the situation and Missy was hauled away in an ambulance, I made my second of four broadcasts. I dedicated the break to Missy Lingner by talking only about the inflatable Miller Lite chair. My great hope was that the ambulance radio was tuned to 93.1 FM.

THE STARSTRUCK GROUPIE

—

"**BE CAREFUL, DOC,**" Hot Rod said. "Radio fans can be real scary. They can get obsessed. And they always sound more attractive than they actually are. Just like us jocks."

There was a rule among radio professionals to never break character with listeners, never get personal with them, never eat the baked goods they sent to the station—and there were always baked goods sent to the station—and never, ever date a listener. Even fucking a listener was discouraged.

Long after Allison and I had broken up and during one of the stretches when we weren't speaking, I began getting calls from a listener who wanted to set me up with her friend, also a listener. The friend loved my voice. She thought I was funny and really knew my music. And thanks to the station's website, which had pictures of all the staff, she thought I was cute.

By now, I was on-air full time. The majority of the work had me reporting traffic, which included morning- and afternoon-shift sidekick duties. I was also jocking a weekend day shift and weekend overnights and filling in on any other dayparts when needed. The phone calls would come at least once a week directly to me through the traffic hotline when I was up at the new traffic studios in the old *Live! From Las Vegas* space at the Stratosphere. If I was covering the midday or afternoon shift down in the full studio, the friend would call the studio hotline. On the occasions when I was jocking my weekend shift live, she'd catch me on the studio hotline then, too. It seemed that this girl listened to me on the radio more than I was actually on the radio.

I was flattered, of course. Who wouldn't be? I still had a wounded heart from my time with Allison, and the flattery and flirtation were good medicine. Plus, the friend sounded cute. I knew better, but my ego and hormones knew best. After several weeks of these calls and brief conversations, I asked why the friend who had the crush on me wasn't the one actually calling. Because she was shy, I was told. I don't like shy girls, I said. She'd call me herself next time, the friend said. Yeah, it was all very junior high.

In my new position, I was no longer in the station as much during bank hours. I had successfully avoided seeing and speaking to Allison for about two months when I ran into her at the station while doing prep for my weekend show before heading up to the Strat for the afternoon shift.

"Hi," she said.

"Hey."

"I've been listening to you every day."

"Thanks."

"You sound great. You're really coming into your own."

"Thanks."

"Are you seeing anyone?"

"No."

"You probably heard that I'm dating Greg."

I hadn't. Greg was one of the sales weasels for KOOL. Slovenly, brash, and obnoxiously confident, I didn't like the guy one bit. And when Allison told me she was dating him, I sure as fuck disliked him even more.

"Why are you telling me this?"

"I wanted you to hear it from me. Not let it fester as a rumor. I figured that would be easier."

"Okay. I'm on my way out, so…"

"It was nice seeing you."

"Okay."

In the middle of the shift, the traffic hotline rang. I answered.

"KOOL Traffic."

"Dr. Dave?"

"Yeah."

"This is Leyla. My friend Jen has been talking to you about me?"

It was a busy afternoon, and I was about to go on-air, so it took me a minute to put the two together. "Oh yeah. Sure. The one who has a little crush on me."

She giggled bashfully. "Yeah."

"Hang on a second." I put the phone down, threw on my headphones, quickly checked the status of the Nevada Highway Patrol traffic log, glanced at the main highways from my view at the Strat, turned my mic on, waited for T.J. Thompson to throw it to me and then gave my report. When I finished, I turned off the mic, took off the headphones and picked up the phone. "Sorry 'bout that. How are you? Leyla, right?"

"That was so cool. I was listening to you actually give the report, *and* I could hear it on my car radio. So cool."

"Technology, baby."

"I know you don't like shy girls, so I'm just going to come right out with it. Would you like to go out with me?"

I had never been on a blind date before. I had never had any interest in going on a blind date. But I was shaken by running into Allison earlier that day and the news that she had a new boyfriend. I was hurt and desperate. All reason and good judgment went out the window. The lyrics of The Beach Boys' "Help Me Rhonda" filled my head:

Well since she put me down I've been out doin' in my head
Come in late at night and in the mornin' I just lay in bed
Well, Rhonda you look so fine (look so fine)
And I know it wouldn't take much time
For you to help me Rhonda
Help me get her out of my heart

"Sure," I said.

"Really?"

"Why not. Your friend did a great job of talking you up. Yeah, let's do it. Got plans tomorrow night?"

"No. I'm totally open."

We decided to meet at a Chinatown bar. I voicetracked my overnight show in case things ran late. Plus, my friend Ben Fowler's birthday party was happening at the Icehouse, a bar and live music venue downtown, and in case things weren't working out, I could reduce the awkwardness by bringing her to the social scramble that would be Ben's party. A new band was playing called The Killers.

I asked her what she looked like so I would recognize her when she arrived. Jen had said countless times that she was blond and cute, but I wanted to hear specifics from the source.

"I'm petite. But I have an hourglass shape. I have short, blond hair, big blue eyes and a big smile. I know what you look like, so I'll find you if you don't recognize me."

Her physical description sounded enticing. Just different enough from Allison to not be Allison, but similar enough to fulfill what I missed about Allison—she was a woman. Her voice was raspy, like Stevie Nicks, and sweetly flirtatious. When the short phone call was over, I was actually excited about the date's potential.

I got to the bar early. Enough for two beers. I had forgotten to grab a snack or a small dinner, so the two beers were making their unfettered way through my blood. The bar was mostly empty. Just me, an older Asian couple and a standard Vegas burnout hunched over a bar-top video poker machine. A young woman walked in. I knew right away that it was Leyla. She was short, as she described, had tight, curly blond hair that stopped just below her chin, as she described. What I couldn't make out was the hourglass shape she had described. As she walked toward me, I quickly played Tetris with her body to see from what angle that shape would appear. Her body looked more like a beach ball with arms and legs than anything else. Her blue eyes and smile were big, and I thought that there was something pretty about her. Maybe it was the pound of makeup she wore. I thought, this is why I didn't do blind dates—they create warped assumptions and hopes that are easily extinguished when you meet so that the date begins with vain disappointment. I wouldn't have been disappointed had she been honest in the first place. Petite doesn't mean short. It didn't matter. We were on the date. This was happening.

"Hi, Dr. Dave."

"Leyla."

We shook hands and ordered a round of drinks. Another beer for me. She had a rum and Coke. The conversation was polite small talk. Her shyness was apparent. I immediately felt that she was in awe of me and had spent all of her bravery asking me out on that phone call. I was getting uncomfortable and began drinking faster. I ordered two more. She wasn't offering much to the conversation, answering my questions with as few words as possible. To fill the awkward spaces, I talked. And I talked and I talked and I talked. She smiled. She winked when I said clever things. I guess she was flirting. I don't know; I was drunk.

I determined that we needed to go to Ben's party and see this band. We asked the bartender for the tab. I reached for it.

"No please, let me," she said. "I insist. It's not every day I get to have drinks and conversation with a celebrity."

I laughed before realizing she wasn't kidding. She was starstruck by me.

We drove to the Icehouse separately. Inside, I quickly found my friends and told Ben, "I'm on this blind date, and I'm bored out of my mind." His response was to hand me a martini. Leyla switched to martinis, too. I introduced her to my friends, but she remained shy and starstruck, which made my friends laugh. As her buzz kicked in, she became clingier, trying to hold my hand, telling me how cute I was, rubbing my back as we talked to people. During the show, she stood in front of me and pressed her body into mine. I was outpacing her two-to-one. I was too drunk, too confused, and maybe even too polite to reject what I assumed were her advances. And I was worried about losing a listener to a broken heart.

When the show ended, I was just barely maintaining control of my limbs. In the parking lot I told her, "You're going to have to drive me home." We got into her car. The radio was set to 93.1 FM, of course. It was after midnight, and I was on the air.

"Oh my God! It's you! This is so weird. How do you do that? You recorded it earlier? I mean, of course you did. Is that so you could be with me tonight?"

"Uh huh."

"Wow. That's so amazing. That's so sweet. You are so amazing and sweet." The next song to play was Aretha Franklin's "(You Make Me Feel Like) A Natural Woman." "Oh my God! I love this song. How did you know that?"

"I didn't." I felt my stomach churn. "You should probably get me home."

She sang along. Sort of. She was off pitch, behind, then ahead, of tempo. I don't know how she wasn't embarrassed by it, but I had only enough sobriety left in me to be embarrassed for her. When the song ended, she said, "I want to be a singer. I want to perform in lounges. That's why I'm in Las Vegas."

"Where'd you come from?"

"Barstow."

Then she leaned over and kissed me. I let it happen. Too drunk to push back. I needed the ride home. My friends had all left, and taxis in Las Vegas don't go off-Strip.

I directed her to my neighborhood, but I didn't want her to know where I lived, so I got us a little lost. My hope was that she would drive in circles long enough to get bored or frustrated and take me up on my offer to "Just drop me off here. I'll find my way home. It's getting late. You should go."

"I'm not going to leave you. You're so drunk, you don't even know how to tell me how to get to your house. How are *you* going to find it?"

Yeah, I hadn't thought that part through, I guess. And so, I gave in, and we arrived at my door. I blacked out upon arrival. I do, however, remember moments... Flashes of her pale, chubby, naked body, no hourglass shape in sight or feel. I remember struggling with the condom. I remember being bored as she had her way with me. I remember that she sang "Killing Me Softly" after she came. It was fucking weird. And again, really pitchy.

I woke up in bed alone the next morning with a headache and bulk amount of self-loathing but a sense of relief big enough to fill all of the Las Vegas Valley. I dragged myself to the bathroom to pee, drink some water, and swallow three ibuprofen pills. Then I went back to bed and slept until two in the afternoon.

By then, I felt strong enough and unlikely to puke enough to go downstairs and make some breakfast before anchoring myself to the couch for an afternoon of TV and napping. At some point, I would have to call a friend for a lift to get my car, but there was no rush. I wasn't going anywhere soon.

I heard the television when I opened my bedroom door and stepped into the hallway. I didn't remember turning the TV on with Leyla the night before, but hell, there was probably a lot we did that I didn't remember. Halfway down the steps, I saw why the TV was on. Sitting on my couch wearing the same stone-washed, high-waisted jeans, and white bodysuit from last night with her thick makeup still mostly intact was Leyla.

"What the fuck are you doing?"

"Well, good morning, sunshine!"

"No. What the fuck are you doing?"

"I'm sorry. Did the TV wake you?"

"No. Why in the fuck are you still here?"

"I was waiting for you to wake up so we could go get your car."

"You've been watching TV in my house all day?"

"I didn't want to wake you. You were pretty drunk last night. I figured you needed to sleep it off."

"What the fuck are you doing here?"

"You left your car at the Icehouse last night. I'll take you back to get it."

"No. I have friends that can do that. You don't need to be here."

"Do you want me to leave?"

She seemed offended, and I immediately felt guilty. My mother had raised me to be a better host than this. I tuned down my rhetoric. "Let's go get my car. I'll go get dressed."

I returned to my room and shut the door behind me. I desperately wanted to shower the night away but was far more desperate to get that girl out of my house. Her intentions seemed sweet but seeing her there really freaked me out. And when I thought about how starstruck she had been the night before and considered how she had her friend calling me on the radio for her, it freaked me out even more. I worried that I might never get rid of this girl. She knows where I live now. She probably knows my real name. Who knows what she dug through in the twelve hours during which I was passed out. I checked my wallet. The cash and credit cards were still there. But maybe she had written the card information down. Had she found my checkbook in my office desk drawer?

Just as I started to slip into the boxer shorts that had been ripped off and flung across the room during the leadup to sex, Leyla barged in. She soaked up my nakedness as I stood there surprised.

"Mmmm. Now that looks like a healthy breakfast." She advanced.

"No! We're leaving."

We drove to the Icehouse listening to KOOL. Neither of us said a word. Thankfully, she only hummed instead of singing along. She pulled up next to my car in the otherwise vacant gravel parking lot. I thanked her for the evening and for the ride. She tried to kiss me. I deflected with, "Best not to. I could puke at any moment."

SHE CALLED THE TRAFFIC LINE a few times after that over the next few weeks. There was no caller-ID so I was never sure when it was her, and I had to answer the phone in order to do my job. I learned that she would frequently call between three-forty-five and four o'clock in the afternoon. Any call that came in during that fifteen-minute period went ignored. Eventually, they stopped coming. She never emailed me, and I never saw her at any remote events or KOOL-sponsored concerts. She must have understood that what we had was all we were going to have. And I respect her tenacity and her subsequent understanding.

But for a while, I was nervous whenever I went out. The problem with being a radio personality on a top-three-ranked station is that people listen to you, get to know you and like you. And they have access to you. A scorned lover or obsessed fan can always be where you are because you have to tell listeners where you're going as a way of getting them to join you. Much of the success of the station depends on sponsored appearances. On top of that, Leyla knew where I lived and what kind of car I drove and what I looked like naked and had spent twelve hours in my house while I was unconscious. She had the upper hand, the higher ground.

I broke the cardinal rule of being a radio jock and risked my life as a result. For as easily as Leyla went away, I could have just as easily ended up a prisoner in her Las Vegas apartment where she would make me jock her own in-home karaoke performances. Like *Misery* but with an out-of-tune soundtrack.

LIVE! WITH DR. DAVE MAXWELL

YOU MIGHT NOT THINK IT, but working the overnight shift on an oldies radio station was thrilling. Overnights in Las Vegas were busy, and KOOL had one of the strongest signals in the Valley, so we were able to reach cars and trucks and small towns and large trailer parks as well as the graveyard-shift workers and gamblers and night owls who occupied them far beyond the glimmer of the Las Vegas Lights. The music and I became part of their routine, and whenever I jocked the show live, I gladly took their calls and their requests.

Working the overnight shift was an exercise in public solitude. The station building on Desert Inn Road was dark and quiet. The voicetracked shows of the other stations played low from their studios with the doors propped open so the one weekend graveyard-shift engineer could keep a sleepy ear trained for the sudden sound of silence and swiftly react to put the station, whichever station it was, back on the air or call in the reinforcements—the varsity team, the daily, full-time engineers. Mostly, he stayed put in another sister station's studio—KWNR, the country station—where he surfed the web and dozed off and on. He'd make rounds every hour or so, and I always caught him off guard when he'd enter the KOOL studio to find me manning the board. What sort of twentysomething would waste a perfectly good Saturday night in Las Vegas behind a microphone and digital records listening to music that hadn't seen the top—or bottom—of a chart in three decades?

Me. That's who. Dr. Dave Maxwell.

On those nights, I had the run of the company. The overnight engineer and I gave each other an exceptionally wide berth. He had his routine, and I had mine. I'd get there an hour before midnight with a six-pack of beer and tacos. I'd eat and drink while touching up the show prep I'd worked on earlier in the week.

There's no feeling quite like one song coming to an end as you place your cans over your ears, turn on your microphone, push its volume up and fire off the next song as you begin talking in a calculated race to the post—the point where the instrumental introduction ends and the lyrics begin. You have to be careful not to step on the singer's first note and just as careful not to leave too much space before that. Timing is everything in radio. If you're a millisecond off, you can botch the entire break; screw up the promo, confuse the listener or even lose the listener altogether. Every time I went live like this, I gave into my instincts.

I didn't think about it. The thinking part was already done; this was the time for jocking. My father, who had been a guest in the studio a few times while I worked, would make fun of me. The way I bounced in the chair or danced and rocked and weaved after pushing the chair back, the way I ducked and dodged at the microphone like a welterweight fighter avoiding punches to the rhythm of the song and the words I needed to say. When it was time to move from song to song or into and out of a break or give the weather report or—whatever—I was part of the song, the promo, the music bed. It was symbiotic. I wasn't aware of how I looked, and it didn't matter. This was radio. All that mattered was the sound. If I looked like a waterhead having a seizure while making good radio, so be it. Sure, my dad made fun of me, but he was also proud of me, and that mattered a whole hell of a lot more than any sort of graceful physical behavior.

Going live always jacked up the nerves. That could have been part of my awkward dancing—my shucking and jiving, as Hot Rod called it. Perhaps I was excising nervous energy. I once asked Hot Rod if he ever got nervous when he went live. "If I didn't, I wouldn't do this," he answered. There was nothing like live radio. Nothing like controlling it, like being it. Nothing.

It's amazing the kind of information I learned to cram into an eight-second walk-up. Car giveaway promo? Yep. Push the weekday morning show? That, too. Humorous commentary on a hot news item? Absolutely. History of the song? You bet your ass. Squeeze in a short chat with a listener and their request? Definitely. And when I was faced with a longer intro, like the twenty-seven seconds on The Hollies' "Long Cool Woman in a Black Dress," the infinite opportunities of the universe were mine. Unlike high school, however, I couldn't just run my mouth off. I had to have twenty-seven seconds' worth of something to say. And when you're a lonely radio DJ talking to countless faceless and nameless people, twenty-seven seconds is a lifetime. But it goes by faster than you think twenty-seven seconds could ever go, and yet, it is packed with more immediate and exploding excitement than any lifetime could hold each and every time.

If the calls were light, I'd solicit my friends to make requests for the songs coming up in the playlist. One good buddy of mine, Billy Lawrence, loved this. I always thought he'd make a mint in the voice-actor business because he had a thousand screwy ways to manipulate his vocal cords. And he could throw those voices at me at any given call no matter the time of night.

My friends became the most important element to the *Dr. Dave Maxwell Show*. They helped me create an experience that was highly curated but 100 percent organic at the same time. I'd have them stop by the station and would put them on-air. I'd give them faux identities of the Las Vegas night: cab drivers and bartenders getting off shift, dealers just starting their day. My pal Joey DeFrancesco was most often game for this. A fellow oldies music geek, he, I think, really wanted to be a radio DJ instead of a TV camera man. Or maybe both. And he would have been great at it because his voice was incredibly smooth. He bought a nice house with money made from the voiceover work he did on the side.

Because I was the weekend overnight jock, I had to continue the voicetracked New Year's Eve party. We recorded the countdown and the party leading up to it a few days before December 31. The morning show hosted it, but the entire KOOL staff was there. And though it was being recorded days before New Year's Eve and in the middle of the day, there was plenty of food and drink, and we partied hard. We ran it in the three hours leading up to midnight, which was when my shift began. It was then my job to continue the illusion. And though I wasn't a big fan of faking it, I voicetracked it. I called my friends into the studio on a night when Coyote's evening voicetracked show was running. I provided the beer and champagne, and Joey sprung for the pizza. I told him not to. I told him the station would pay for it, but he insisted. Joey, like many of my friends, just wanted to be a part of the radio experience.

On really slow nights—the nights when people weren't calling in and my friends weren't around to fake excitement and requests for me—I would occasionally voicetrack an hour or two ahead of the clock. It was a process that took about twenty minutes. That would give me enough time to run out to Chinatown for a thirty-minute massage or a dim sum meal. I'd return to the studio with a fresh pack of beer, released, relaxed still slick with baby oil, and reinvigorated, ready to finish out my show.

My only regret as an overnight jock was that I never got the Suicide Call. It's not that I wanted people to kill themselves, but the late-night call of desperation to the adored radio host was a tall tale I wanted to experience. I always figured that it would happen to me. I mean, I was in Las Vegas, with the strongest signal in the Valley. Things get ominous and strange out there in the middle of the dark and lonely desert. And I operated in good times and great oldies—the bygone past. In the depths of personal sadness, it can feel like the only person listening is the guy you're listening to. I was primed for late night, substance-abused melancholy. But it never came.

And that's a good thing, right? Because I knew plenty of people who blew their brains out or ate too many pills or drank too many cocktails *by design*. But I wonder... if they had called me and I took their request and played their favorite song just for them, whether they'd have felt like they mattered enough to make it through the bleak night to the opportunities presented with a new day.

Then again, maybe that call did come. I just wasn't there because I had voicetracked the show so that I could slouch over a bar and try to get laid. When my time comes, I look forward to asking God—if He or She exists—how many souls came His or Her way because I didn't answer the KOOL 93.1 hotline.

The drive home at six in the morning was the perfect winddown for a few hours of sleep before rejoining the day dwellers for a movie or dinner with friends or a swim in my pool. It was during these overnight shows and early morning drives that I found perfect comfort in brand-new dawn solitude. I had listeners, sure, but the majority of the world was sleeping while I was up making radio, experiencing an adrenaline rush of bursting star power every few minutes. I was producing, while the rest of the world was consuming or dreaming. It was a superior feeling.

The power, the influence that a radio DJ wields was never lost on me. And I never took it for granted.

—
DEAD
AIR
—

TOM DENIS AND I HAD BEEN PALS from when I was Allison's assistant, and he was the cluster's production assistant. The reality was that he handled 90 percent of the work that came through because the production director spent 90 percent of his time standing in the middle of the parking lot smoking Pall Malls. But working closely as Clear Channel Las Vegas' two traffic reporters in the Stratosphere studio for two years turned us into good friends.

At Christmastime, we decorated the studio with lights and a small plastic tree. We put our names in a hat and drew for Secret Santa, impressing ourselves with how funny we were since it was just the two of us and there was no secret, of course. We threw mini birthday parties for each other. We instituted theme days. There were Movie Mondays, when one of us would bring in a DVD and we'd watch it on my laptop in the three- or five-minute increments between our respective broadcast times. And there were Thirsty Thursdays, when we'd either bring in a case of beer or buy tall cans from the gift shop and drink during the last hour of the afternoon shift. In the summer, Thursdays became Thrill-Ride Thursdays, when we'd drink as usual before heading off to one of the rides at the Strat or the rollercoasters at New York-New York or Circus Circus. After bungee jumping during one of those Thursdays, that became the standard.

Tom was the friend who helped me get through some of the hardest parts with Allison. He calmed me down, talked me up and since he was a few years older, shared stories of his own heartbreak and recovery. When his daughter was born just an hour before the morning shift, I covered for him, then bolted to the hospital to meet the little squirt the moment I got off the air. I took on his shifts as well as mine for the week he stayed home to get used to his new parental role. When I took two weeks off to travel to Australia, Tom was upset with me when I returned. Not because of the workload he had to juggle along with being a new dad to a kid who wouldn't sleep through the night but because he missed me.

It was a great gig. We worked the split shift, and after the morning drive was done, we'd grab breakfast at the Stratosphere's employee dining room. That gave us the middle of the day to nap, run errands, swim in our respective backyard pools or do whatever we wanted. Sometimes I'd get to squeeze in a remote, which meant more money—which was always desperately needed. Sometimes I'd fill in on the midday shift, which meant that I was on-air for the three most-listened-to shifts of the five dayparts. I was getting an incredible amount of air-time between the traffic, the fill-ins, the remotes and my weekend shifts. I had become KOOL's most frequently heard personality. There's even an argument that I was accumulating the most air-time logged of any jock in all of Las Vegas radio. It was probably overkill but as long as the ratings remained high, which they did, it was hard to argue with it. If the money had been better, it would have been completely perfect.

I don't say this to brag or to make you think that I was some kind of a big deal—I was an M-list celebrity at best. I tell you this so that you understand that I was living a certain stage of my dream. Somewhere just after larva and approaching pupa. I was working hard and getting better at it, and I figured the money would come. More opportunities would come. That's what I'd always been taught, anyway.

But as I was living it up, insidious business moves were being made. Despite the success of the cluster over all, the longtime general manager was fired without warning and replaced by a younger woman named Trina Lowell. I liked

Trina. She was smart and funny. But I did not completely trust Trina. It felt to me, and many others in the building, that she was a willing pawn of Clear Channel Corporate. Her ascent to the position was not natural. She was barely in her thirties and had only spent a little time as a sales manager in San Antonio, where Clear Channel was headquartered. A rumor made its way around the office that she had slept her way to the top. I never really bought into that theory. I figured it was more that she was good at her job and that Corporate wanted an intelligent and reliable GM who was more agreeable to their whims. They found that in Trina. The other benefit for the company was that this change was an obvious move to better diversify Clear Channel's leadership. They wanted to see more women in top roles. And they tasked their new golden girl with getting the Las Vegas cluster to cut costs and skew younger.

There was no sound reason for this other than good, old-fashioned American greed. All of the cluster's stations were holding strong in the ratings and bringing in those sales dollars. I understand that in business, the target audience is the youth market. But that's the benefit of owning four stations in a single market. Clear Channel had all the demographics covered between KOOL, Sunny, KWNR, and KWID Wild 102, the rhythmic CHR station. But none of that mattered. Trina's orders had been given, her battle axe was drawn, and heads needed to roll.

Hot Rod was the first to go. Trina wanted KOOL to shift its programming to include mid-to-late '70s and even some early '80s tunes. Hot Rod was the most outspoken against her mandated adjustments to the format, and he was the highest paid person on staff after her. He didn't even get a chance to say goodbye. There was no formal farewell party honoring him for his years of service and his leadership that brought the company one of the highest rated oldies channels in the nation and the largest, most successful single radio station promotion in Las Vegas history—maybe in radio history. Nothing.

The way he explained it to me when he called me from his cell phone after being escorted out of the station by hotsheet rent-a-cops was that Trina came into his office with Cathy, the head of human resources, closed the door and told him he needed to pack his personals. It was in the middle of his voicetracked shift. He didn't even get to give one final farewell to the listeners. He drove home, fired after a decade of providing bold, original, and financially lucrative programming, listening to the station he built as his own beautiful voice walked up the intro to his favorite Beach Boys song, "Wouldn't It Be Nice." The irony, he said, is what stung the most.

His replacement was there the next day. The office had been painted overnight, and new furniture had been moved in. It did not look like the office of a radio program director.

It looked like a photograph from an OfficeMax catalogue. The stooge's name was Art Mason. His dress and grooming choices made him look like your depressed, divorced dad. He also took over the midday shift, and it sounded just as flat and void of personality as his office looked. The kind of radio your depressed, divorced dad would love. Art didn't understand the format; he didn't know the music or the lifestyle, and I don't think he cared. But he was my boss, and I managed to get along with him as much as I needed to. After all, I had a job to do and a career metamorphosis to consider.

However, my frustration grew when he fired T.J. and brought in Johnny 'The J-Man' Stevens to temporarily fill the slot. The J-Man was someone Art had worked with at his last station in Tampa—an adult-contemporary station like Sunny. He sounded like anybody else doing their cheesiest impression of a coked-up '80s radio jock. But he wasn't kidding. He knew less about the music than Art did, and his board work was routinely incoherently sloppy. Often, I would get through half of my traffic reports before he realized he didn't have my mic turned on back in the studio. The J-Man was an embarrassment to the profession and an insult to the format.

I wanted that afternoon drive shift. I had worked hard for it. I had name recognition and ratings to prove that I could carry it. I knew the format and had filled in at least two dozen times before. Plus, I didn't run the board with my elbows and ass, which is what I assumed The J-Man was doing. Pardon my bravado, but I was the reasonable heir apparent to T.J. Thompson. I submitted my interest to Art both formally through the application process and informally in his office during the midday break between my traffic shifts. He, too, had voicetracked the midday, but unlike Hot Rod, he did not listen to his show. He didn't even listen to the station. There was no stereo in his office.

"Don't you want to listen to the station? Don't you need to monitor it?" I asked while sitting across from him in his OfficeMax office.

"Oh, I am," he said.

I sat quietly to see if I could hear some low volume from maybe a small stereo under his desk. "How?"

He turned his computer monitor toward me. "I'm streaming it through the web. See those EQ bars? As long as those are moving, I know we're still on the air. So, what did you want to talk to me about?"

"The afternoon shift."

"Ah, yes. You'd be great in that slot."

"You think?"

"Of course, I do. You have a great presence on the microphone. You know your stuff, and the listeners love you."

"Thank you. I'm so happy to hear you say that, Art. Because I want to take the success TJ. built and work with you to build even more."

"I think that's a fantastic idea."

"Does this mean that—?"

"But you're doing such an incredible job where you're at now. We don't need to shake up the traffic or the weekends."

"I could still do the weekends."

"J-Man will be moving into the slot permanently. Effective today."

It was a blow. A combination throat and gut punch, followed by a roundhouse kick with his loafers straight in my 'nads. I walked out of his office defeated.

From there, Art amped up the dismantling of KOOL. He shifted the format much closer to adult-contemporary, which did not sit well with the folks at Sunny, so Trina had them shift hotter and frighteningly closer to Top 40 CHR, which began to butt up against what Wild was doing. It was hardly surprising when Tom and I arrived at the Stratosphere one morning, turned on the stations and no longer heard Wild but the Guns 'n' Roses' song "Welcome to the Jungle" playing on repeat, and an email to the Clear Channel Communications Las Vegas cluster informing us that KWID Wild 102 would be transitioning to KWID, La Preciosa 101.9 FM, a Spanish AC channel. Ah yes, there was one demographic that Clear Channel hadn't touched—the Latinos.

La Preciosa would be a satellite station. All of the talent was being provided by voicetracked talent spread throughout the country. Marketing was handled at the corporate level and through whatever sales packages the sales team could piece together. This meant, of course, that everyone at KWID was canned, save for those on the sales team who could speak Spanish or were willing to learn it within a month. A small team of young Latino men were hired to set up remote broadcasts and hand out station swag when needed.

Trina purchased a ton of TV spots to announce and promote the change via well-placed billboards at almost every intersection throughout the Valley. I had only been working in professional radio for five years at that point, but I knew that this effort was futile. There was always an initial spike in the ratings when a station flipped. Curiosity of the shiny new thing is human nature. But eventually, people would get bored and want something they could relate to. When that became impossible for them, they would change channels. Radio had always been more than the content coming through the speakers. It had been about the people behind the microphones and the control boards creating that content and turning it into the human experience.

IT WAS A RARE, gloomy Saturday in Las Vegas. I was jocking my day shift live. I always preferred to dim the lights in the studio to make it feel more like a performance space rather than a fluorescent-lighted drunk tank. The KOOL studio was across from Wild–turned-La Preciosa, and I used to get a kick out of writing insulting messages on pieces of paper and holding them up for the Wild weekend jock to see. She was a sassy lady, about a decade older than me named Gina Gee. She'd reciprocate. Even on the quiet weekends, there was always a shared excitement about what we were doing that coursed through the hallways of the building. But on that Saturday, I stared into an empty, lifeless studio window and saw nothing more than the dim glow of the channel buttons on the board casting just enough light for me to make out the Wild 102, "Where Hip Hop Lives!" banner hanging from the wall by one corner grommet. The studio—the station—had been abandoned. The listeners had been abandoned. And soon enough, the new listeners would realize that there was nothing there for them either. Within four years, Clear Channel would sell off La Preciosa.

The ship was sinking. Like any rat with half a brain, I knew I needed to get out. With my prospects dashed for advancement at KOOL, or anywhere within the Clear Channel Las Vegas cluster, I started looking for jobs at other companies. A few program directors took my calls or met me for lunch, but no one was hiring. I looked for opportunities all over the country. Gigs as an on-air host, a traffic reporter, a marketing guy, a board operator. I descended through my radio résumé in hopes that if I cast enough lines with all of my bait, I'd catch something, and I'd be able to get myself back where I wanted to be. I came across plenty of voicetracking shifts. But with so many more experienced DJs also trawling for work, I was unable to land a single overnight shift in even the smallest of markets. The sea of opportunity had been fished to death.

A NEW CONCEPT RESTAURANT AND BAR had opened up at one of the local casinos off the Strip. As usual, media was invited to the soft opening as a way to get us all excited about it and begin building the buzz. Ben, as a member of the print media, met me there. As was the case with these kinds of events, in attendance were my three favorite Las Vegas celebrity blowhards.

Monti Rock III. A guy who managed to build and mostly maintain a career of odd celebrity who was so committed to self-adulation that he had his Dodge Neon wrapped in a cartoonish design displaying his name and face. It was a questionable move because his status took a few hits in my book when I saw that car parked on the street outside of a dingy apartment complex on the city's west side where he lived.

John Di Domenico. An impersonator who was making his big splash portraying Austin Powers. This guy was making a living impersonating a character played by an actor from a movie that was, at that time, eight years old.

And Robin Leach. The 1980s-television-personality-turned-Las-Vegas-gossip-columnist who could have held the title of Handsiest and Creepiest Old Perverted Drunk in Las Vegas. But that award belonged to Las Vegas Mayor Oscar Goodman, the mob defense attorney-turned-politician. And yeah, Mayor Goodman was there, too, with a fully costumed showgirl on each arm and a martini in each hand. As always.

I was in a horrible mood that night. Ben and I slouched at the bar and sucked back beer; me complaining about things; him listening. It was a social event, but neither of us felt like being social, so it was a little unnerving when I was tapped on the shoulder by someone saying my name. I turned around. It was Allison.

It had been months since I'd seen her. I was hopeful that I wouldn't have had to again. But this is Las Vegas. It's a small town, and come on, what did I really think would happen? That I'd go to a media event with free food and drink, one she was certainly invited to as well, and not see her? Come on, Dr. Dave…

"Hi," she said.

"Hey," I said.

"Hi, Ben."

"Allison."

"I'm sorry about the afternoon shift," she said to me.

"What about it?"

"I heard that you talked to Art about it."

"How did you hear that?"

"I don't know. You know how word gets around that place."

Then her new boyfriend, that sonofabitch Greg, walked up behind her with drinks in his hand. He wrapped his arm around her to hand off her glass of red wine.

"Oh, hey, Dr. Dave! What's up, man?" He reached out to shake my hand. The guy had no idea how much I hated his fucking guts. I shook it anyway.

"Greg."

"Who's this?" he asked, thrusting his hand out to Ben. "I'm Greg. You a friend of Dr. Dave's?" Ben, God love him, didn't shake his hand. He coughed and said, "Yep. My best buddy right here," then took a long drink from his beer, staring him down the entire time. The awkwardness was not lost on any of us except Greg. "Great!" he said.

"What are you drinking there?" Ben asked Greg.

"A frozen strawberry margarita."

"Ah-ha. The tropical drink perfect for a Las Vegas nightclub opening in February. Cool, man. Cool."

"Right on! Oh, hey, there's Monti Rock. Allison, I'm gonna go try to talk to him. I *love* that guy! He drives the coolest car!"

Greg turned and made his way to Monti Rock, who was cradling his stuffed cat toy. As Greg walked away, I noticed that the back of his white dress shirt was drenched in sweat. Allison noticed it, too.

"Did you spill a drink down his back?" I asked.

"No."

"Did he?"

Ben laughed, then turned back to the bar and ordered us another round of free drinks.

"Listen, can we go somewhere and talk?" Allison asked me.

"About what?"

"There's just… I just feel like things ended strange with us and I… I don't know. I miss you, and I'd love to talk to you about a few things."

I could tell she had had enough of Greg. But did she want me back? Was that what this was about? It didn't matter. I knew I couldn't even begin to entertain the idea. We had had our fun, and we had had our misery. I learned that there was not enough conceding I could do to make any kind of relationship with Allison function, and there was not enough alcohol in the world to get me through another breakup. This was the end for me. Things had run their course. When it came to Allison, I was a rock, an island. I was living the words of Simon & Garfunkel.

"I don't think that's a good idea," I said. "Ben and I are in the middle of something here. And you should probably go make sure Greg doesn't end up giving Monti Rock a handjob."

She turned around and saw her boyfriend with the sweaty goatee and the sweat-soaked dress shirt and the suburban-housewife cocktail falling all over himself while talking to an old queen who could not look less interested. "Yeah," she sighed. "Maybe I could call you later then?"

"Probably not."

The expression on her face looked like what I imagine mine did when Art told me The J-Man got the afternoon shift. I didn't want to hurt her; I just didn't want to have anything to do with her.

"Okay," she said. "Well, you guys have fun. Nice seeing you, Ben." He barely smiled and nodded. "I guess, maybe I'll see you around the station sometime, David."

"Okay."

The next morning I told Tom about the encounter.

"Good for you, man. Good for you. How do you feel?"

"I feel better than I've felt in years. Like the dead weight has been cut from my ankles, and I can finally swim again."

"Yep. The only better feeling than falling in love is the feeling you get when you realize that you're finally over it."

After we had our breakfast, I headed into the station. Art was in the studio voicetracking his show. I walked in and sat in the chair across from him. I saw Allison burn past the window. It was the walk I'd seen a million times before—she was headed to chew someone out.

"Uh, Dave. I'm recording here," Art said.

"This will only take a moment.

"Go on."

"I'm resigning."

"What?"

"I quit."

"You can't quit. You're an integral part of this station."

"No, I'm not. Not anymore. Come on, Art. Don't make this harder for me than it already is. I loved this job, this station, this place. But I can't do this anymore. There's nothing here for me, and I can't give it anything. You won't let me. So I quit."

"If you quit now, you know you can't do your shift this afternoon."

"I know."

"Or your weekend shifts."

"Yeah, I know. That's what quitting is." I reached into my shoulder bag and handed him my resignation letter. I had been carrying it around for six weeks—written the night Art told me I wouldn't be the afternoon host. "I'll run another copy up to Cathy in HR. Good luck with everything."

As I pulled out of the station parking lot, I cried. Bawled actually. I called Tom. He was probably already napping because the call went right to voicemail. I blubbered through the tears to break the news and let him know he'd be covering my shift that afternoon. Or, what used to be my shift. In a way, it was the last kind of voicetracking I did.

Six weeks later, KOOL flipped formats. Art let the morning show know they were fired by calling their homes and leaving messages on their answering machines. The next day, every bit of oldies evidence was gone. A Top 40 CHR station was there instead, 93.1 The Party. This, like La Preciosa, was a ghost station. The morning show was pumped in from corporate—a new blabberfest featuring unoriginal nonsense from Whoopi Goldberg. Art still voicetracked the midday shift, and The J-Man still barely jocked the afternoon drive. Beyond that, I don't know what they did. I couldn't listen. It was too heartbreaking for me, and frankly, it was just shit radio. And I never once saw them get any TV exposure.

THE WEEK BEFORE MY LAST DAY ON-AIR, in the same studio where my life in radio took off, I saw it: Four fingers, a thumb, a palm. It was the handprint of the guy who threw himself off the top of the Stratosphere; the one Hot Rod told me about but I never believed because I never saw it. But there it was, finally. It was only visible for a moment. The sun revealed it. I froze. Then the sun hid it as it passed along the horizon. Then I yelled through the open door between our studio sections to Tom, "I saw it! The hand!"

"Finally," he said. "I see that damn thing every day."

Why the window washers and the occasional rain hadn't erased it, I couldn't tell you. What I can tell you is that for the next week, I couldn't not see it. And whenever it revealed itself to me, I'd throw up my hand as if I were giving it a high-five.

A farewell salute would have been more appropriate.

BY THE TIME I SAW THE HANDPRINT ON THE WINDOW, it was too late for me. Really, it was too late for radio. Like the jumper who left that print, radio had thrown itself from the highest point into messy irrelevance for the sake of momentary thrills and unsustainable trends. And I helped push it off the edge.

Hadn't I? I helped perfect voicetracking. I was there moving the needle toward the full automation of the medium and the constriction of local influence. I witnessed the corporate greed and shortsightedness that diminished the personality and connective relationship between radio and the listeners and did nothing to stop it. But I couldn't have possibly known where it was all heading—Dr. Dave Maxwell was born of those times. Still, I can't help bear some of the responsibility.

But that's how things go. You can't be a hit forever. You have to take the moments you get and squeeze as much excitement into them as possible making sure to hit that post. That's what a good DJ does. A good DJ leaves you wanting more, has convinced you to follow the command, "Don't touch that dial!" But first, you need a reason to tune in.

THE LAST DJ

SOUNDTRACK

—

COME SEE ABOUT ME	The Supremes
WHOLE LOTTA SHAKIN' GOING ON	Jerry Lee Lewis
HELP ME RHONDA	The Beach Boys
GIVE ME JUST A LITTLE MORE TIME	Chairmen of the Board
RUNAROUND SUE	Dion
SUGAR, SUGAR	The Archies
RUNAWAY	Del Shannon
I AM A ROCK	Simon & Garfunkel
DOMINO	Van Morrison
LUCILLE	Little Richard
YES, I'M READY	Barbara Mason
PAPERBACK WRITER	The Beatles
BRANDY (YOU'RE A FINE GIRL)	Looking Glass
EARTH ANGEL	The Penguins
DON'T YOU CARE	The Buckinghams
BERNADETTE	The Four Tops
THAT'S ALL RIGHT	Elvis Presley
WEDDING BELL BLUES	The 5th Dimension
(I CAN'T GET NO) SATISFACTION	The Rolling Stones
MAYBELLINE	Chuck Berry
MAGGIE MAY	Rod Stewart

Visit Spotify and search The Last DJ playlist or David Himmel to stream and download.

ACKNOWLEDGMENTS

Thanks go to the men and women under the headphones and behind the microphones: Jim Stolz, Shari Schlesinger, Kenneth Emery, Rik Bollman, Mark Melbourne, Robert Grotbeck, Jim Zippo, Diana Kelly and Jonathan Monk, and Michael Hull. You taught me well, were trusted friends, and I hope I made you proud at least once.

Thanks to my wife, Katie Himmel; you help me make art and are a work of art yourself. To the good doctor, Jarret Keene, for the encouragement, friendship, and survival tips. To the literate ape, Don Hall, for the partnership, talks and occasional smokes. And Dana Jerman for the initial read. Thanks to Kate Silver for the eyes and Eric Wilson for the notes. And to Christopher Gallant, Billy Hearth, and Joey DeFrancesco for the calls. Joey D, this mortal coil misses you, my friend. And thanks to Las Vegas for tuning in and listening.

Printed by Amazon Italia Logistica S.r.l.
Torrazza Piemonte (TO), Italy